MURDER, BY ACCIDENT

A Miss Finch Prequel
VIKKI KESTELL

Faith-Filled Fiction™
www.faith-filledfiction.com | www.vikkikestell.com

MURDER BY ACCIDENT

A MISS FINCH PREQUEL
Vikki Kestell
Also Available in eBook Format

———•———

BOOKS BY VIKKI KESTELL

THE TAHOE MYSTERIES
Book 1: *Number 1 with a Bullet*
Book 2: *Be Quick or be Dead*
Book 3: *Death on the Big Blue*, 2026
Murder by Accident, A Miss Finch Prequel

A PRAIRIE HERITAGE
Book 1: *A Rose Blooms Twice*
Book 2: *Wild Heart on the Prairie*
Book 3: *Joy on This Mountain*
Book 4: *The Captive Within*
Book 5: *Stolen*
Book 6: *Lost Are Found*
Book 7: *All God's Promises*
Book 8: *The Heart of Joy*
Book 9: *Rose of RiverBend*

GIRLS FROM THE MOUNTAIN
Book 1: *Tabitha*
Book 2: *Tory*
Book 3: *Sarah Redeemed*

LAYNIE PORTLAND
Book 1: *Laynie Portland, Spy Rising*
Book 2: *Laynie Portland, Retired Spy*
Book 3: *Laynie Portland, Renegade Spy*
Book 4: *Laynie Portland, Spy Resurrected*
Book 5: *Vyper, A Laynie Portland Sequel*

NANOSTEALTH
Book 1: *Stealthy Steps*
Book 2: *Stealth Power*
Book 3: *Stealth Retribution*
Book 4: *Deep State Stealth*
Book 5: *Stealth Insurgence*
Book 6: *Stealth Triumph*
Book 7: *Stealth Genesis*,
     A Nanostealth Prequel

STAND-ALONE BOOKS
I Can't Hear You
The Christian and the Vampire

MURDER
BY ACCIDENT

A MISS FINCH PREQUEL
Vikki Kestell
Also Available in eBook Format

———— o ————

MISS BD FINCH teaches a UCLA course listed in the university catalog as *The Forensics of a Traffic Accident*. As it turns out, not all her case studies are the mishaps they've been labeled.

Rather, while Miss Finch has her students work through each of the six cases, a disturbing trend emerges—a trend that can only be interpreted as carefully staged "hits" *disguised* as accidents. But who is behind this string of connected "accidents"?

As the quarter continues, the students and course TAs cannot help but recognize Miss Finch's methodical unveiling of these concealed crimes . . . nor her deliberate "outing" of the nefarious criminals behind them.

So, is anyone surprised when those criminals come after Miss Finch?

PREPARE YOURSELF FOR . . . **The Tahoe Mysteries**.
Book 1: *Number 1 with a Bullet*
Book 2: *Be Quick or Be Dead*
Book 3: *Death on the Big Blue*, 2026
Murder by Accident, A Miss Finch Prequel

ACKNOWLEDGEMENTS

THANK YOU AS ALWAYS
to my wonderful team,
Cheryl Adkins and **Greg McCann**,
for their loving hearts and
unfailing dedication to this work.

SCRIPTURE QUOTATIONS

COVER DESIGN

Vikki Kestell

———■◆■———

FOREWORD

My Dear Readers,

Murder by Accident is the prequel to my series, *The Tahoe Mysteries*, and introduces you to Miss Finch's back story. However, for maximum enjoyment, I recommend reading the first book of this series, *Number 1 with a Bullet* before reading *Murder by Accident*. I promise you won't regret doing so!

Big hugs,

—Vikki

CHAPTER 1

UNIVERSITY OF CALIFORNIA, LOS ANGELES CAMPUS

WEDNESDAY, WINTER QUARTER, WEEK THREE

MISS BD FINCH, briefcase in one hand, the handle of a rolling pet carrier in the other, approached the main entrance to the DeNeve Commons Lecture Auditorium. Even on UCLA's multifaceted campus, the older woman cut an eye-catching figure: Her mop of wildly curling black hair shot with gray framed an unlined face, yet her most remarked-upon physical characteristics were her deeply hooded brown eyes—compliments of her Korean father—and her height.

Or the lack thereof.

Miss Finch was quite short, you see.

Not a "little person," but definitely on the small side.

Just inside the Commons' entrance, she spied her trio of eager TAs. They were scanning the lobby, awaiting her arrival. They spotted her and sent a unified grin her way, but their outwardly collegial behavior didn't fool her. The three of them were fiercely competitive, each vying, each *determined* (but as unobtrusively as possible) to be the first to anticipate and fulfill her every want or need.

They called to her with one voice, "Good morning, Miss Finch!" even while the two male TAs tussled over the door to the auditorium and who would open it for her.

Miss Finch had an insightful mind. Those who knew her well also freely acknowledged her acerbic, dark-humored wit.

Why, bless their fawning, ambitious little hearts, Lord. My TAs are more entertaining than a chorus of baby birds contending for the same juicy bite of masticated worm.

She chuckled under her breath. *And I, apparently, am the worm—or, at best, the mama bird dispensing treats to her little ones.*

"Let me take that for you, Miss Finch."

Miss Finch had little choice; Miss Zhong, her eager female TA, had snuck in behind her and snatched the briefcase from her hand before Miss Finch realized what was happening.

"Why, *thank* you," she growled.

When one of the male TAs reached for her rolling pet carrier, the index finger of Miss Finch's free hand shot into the air inches from his face. "*No*, thank you . . . Mr. Glenn."

Undeterred, the young Mr. Glenn, a UCLA Bruins' linebacker, elbowed his fellow TA, Mr. Donegal, aside, swung the door to the lecture hall wide, and ushered Miss Finch inside.

She started for her lectern, giving the buzzing auditorium less than a passing glance.

Wait. What?

She stopped and looked a second time. Stared in amazement.

"Mr. Glenn! Mr. Donegal! Miss Zhong!"

Her Three Musketeers scurried to her side. "Yes, Miss Finch?"

Miss Finch turned her back to the auditorium's seating, put both hands on the handle of the rolling pet carrier, and used her chin to gesture them closer.

"Please enlighten me, my amiable, amenable, ardent, and always acquiescent assistants: Just how many students are enrolled in my class?"

"Enrollment is maxed out at one hundred forty, Miss Finch. The class is a mix of pre-med, med, forensics, criminology, and criminal law students. Oh—and seventeen undeclared majors." This stream of consciousness flowed from the enthusiastic Mr. Glenn.

"And this hall seats—?"

"Four hundred thirty max occupancy, Miss Finch," her fawning female TA inserted.

"And yet this room is suspiciously close to capacity this morning, is it not . . . Mr. Donegal?"

Mr. Donegal, whose brain traveled at the speed of light but whose mouth rolled like a cart with square wheels, stammered. "Uh, um, y-y-yes. While enrollment is less than one-third the auditorium's capacity, today's attendance *is* appreciably above enrollment. We seem . . . to have attracted a number of . . . guests. Or visitors? Perhaps they are interested in auditing the class?"

Mr. Glenn was more to the point. "Unless these 'extras' can produce their request to audit the class, they are lurkers. Intruders. Give the word, and I'll clear them out."

Goodness! My kind of gentleman. Miss Finch opened her mouth, but her response was cut off by a strident demand.

"Ms. Finch! *Ms. Finch!*"

The demand issued from none other than Dr. Stanton Normandy, British "expat," professor of criminal law, and director of the program in which Miss Finch's course resided.

"Ah, yes. The principal thorn in my flesh," she muttered under her breath. "How lovely."

The eyes of Miss Finch's TAs narrowed, and they pivoted in unison. Their bodies, ranging in height from one to two heads taller than hers, followed. They halted Dr. Normandy's forward locomotion before he was three strides into the auditorium, forming a cordon between him and his objective.

"Ms. Finch! Really!"

But apparently Miss Finch had contracted a profound—and quite re-cent—hearing loss. Unflustered and unhurried, she rolled her pet carrier up to the auditorium's podium, parked it beside the podium, and stepped up onto the stool behind it. Said stool allowed her to peer over the lec-tern's top at the ocean of young faces before her.

She tapped twice on the live microphone attached to the lectern.

Immediate silence reigned in the auditorium. Those fresh to the class ogled Miss Finch with undisguised curiosity. Her students watched her with avid expectation.

"Good morning, students. I fear I must begin today's class with an indelicate question. Please answer yes or no: Are you Sea Monkeys? And did some injudicious individual add water to our little tank? I ask only because this class's attendance has mysteriously trebled in size."

Her audience laughed, howled, cheered, and elbowed each other.

The very picture of immutable decorum, Miss Finch signaled for si-lence and continued. "For those of you upon whom I have never laid eyes before today, I should state that this course, based on my book of the same name, is *The Forensics of a Traffic Accident.* And, as the flight attendant says when one boards an eastbound flight from LAX, 'If your destination is Hawaii, *you are on the wrong plane.*'"

That earned her another wave of chuckles, but not from Dr. Normandy. Fuming from behind the wall of TAs confounding his every attempt to reach the lectern, he raised his voice. "Really, Ms. Finch! Call off your dogsbodies!"

Miss Finch sighed and said to her students, "One moment, if you please."

At her nod, the TA wall split and Dr. Normandy sailed through. He walked directly to the lectern and muttered, "You have ducked my calls all week, Ms. Finch."

"As today is Wednesday and the time is only 9:00 a.m., I *have not* been ducking your calls 'all week,' as you assert. I *have*, factually, been ducking your calls for less than forty-eight hours, Normandy."

"*Doctor* Normandy, Ms. Finch—and so you do admit to ducking them?"

"*Miss* Finch, *Stanton*—and I admit only to being too busy to indulge in bureaucratic balderdash."

Mr. Glenn tittered. Dr. Normandy whirled on Mr. Glenn and sent a withering glare at the TA who, unflustered, folded his arms across his chest . . . and made his pecs dance.

It was, actually, a quite impressive feat.

Miss Finch clapped a hand over her mouth and resorted to a spate of coughing that, as it went on, could have rivaled a TB ward.

Normandy turned back and drew closer to the lectern. He leaned toward Miss Finch and lowered his voice. "Seeing as how this course is a sad *one-off*, nothing but a misguided *trial*, and seeing as you are *a guest lecturer*, whereas I have oversight of this department's budget, I demand to know how you finagled funding for not *one* but *three* TAs!"

"Funding?" Miss Finch, still struggling to stifle outright laughter, pursed her lips.

Hard.

Harder. Press harder!

Desperate to regain some semblance of composure and needing a distraction to help, she focused her gaze on a lone female student high up in the far right corner of the auditorium. She sent the girl a forced smile and a jaunty little waggle of her fingers. The poor thing sat up straight, jerked her eyes all around her, then pointed to herself and mouthed, "Me?"

Miss Finch nodded.

Blushing and uncertain, the girl waved back.

By then, Miss Finch had herself sorted. "Ah, I see. Funding for three TAs. Yes. Well, in point of fact, Normandy, my TAs are volunteers. All three of them."

Normandy took another step toward her, which put his leg up against the pet carrier and, thanks to the foot-high stool on which the diminutive Miss Finch stood, put him and Miss Finch nearly nose to nose.

Normandy sputtered, "*Volunteer* teaching assistants? I have never heard of such utter nonsense—"

A spitting, snarling yowl against Normandy's left shin startled and galvanized him. He leaped three feet to the side, losing his dignity and very nearly losing his balance. "What in the bloody blue blazes is *that?*"

"*That*, Dr. Normandy, is my precious kittycat."

"You-you-you are *not* allowed to have animals of any kind inside a campus building, Ms. Finch!"

"Hmm. I assure you, *Stanton*, I received a thorough orientation prior to the semester start, and am in complete compliance with UCLA Policy 135: Animals on University Property. I requested and received Assistance Animal status for both my cat and my dog. You do not expect me to leave them home or in my vehicle while I teach, do you? Confined as they are in their carrier, they pose no danger to either students or staff."

Taking care to avoid contact with the pet carrier, Normandy again leaned toward Miss Finch. He did not, however, realize that the lectern mic was and had been picking up their conversation and making it public fare.

"In what universe, pray tell, would *you* require an assistance animal?" he demanded.

She placed both palms on the man's chest, then stepped forward and off the stool, effectively shoving him backward. She stared up at his face. *Way* up.

"You wish to know in what universe *I* would require an assistance animal? Why, in the universe where a five-foot, ten-inch bully such as yourself might encroach upon my personal space. Get in my face like that again, Dr. Normandy, and my assistance cat *will* assist me."

Snickers and guffaws echoed across the auditorium.

Normandy stiffened as he realized the students were watching and listening in. "You . . ." His eyes swept over the auditorium seating… and he wilted. "Wait. This class is capped at one hundred forty. Why is this auditorium near capacity?"

"Why is vanilla the most popular ice cream flavor worldwide? I assume it owes its notoriety to *personal preference*, and I can only assume the same of these students, *Stanton*."

Dr. Normandy drew himself up. "We'll see about that."

"Have at it. By the by, does that mean you're leaving now? Because my class should have commenced three minutes ago."

Normandy turned on his heel and strode from the room, laughter and applause following him out the door. Miss Finch, again wrestling to pull her face into serious lines, stepped up onto her stool and waved for her class to settle down. They did. Although she didn't recognize even half of the faces staring back at her, all of them waited with rapt attention for her to begin.

She had opened her mouth to begin—and she would have begun—had it not been for a small, insidious, two-syllable whisper.

There it was again.

And again!

Within seconds, the whisper grew to a soft chant that was soon picked up across the room.

POUN-cer!

POUN-cer!

POUN-cer!

"Oh, dear. No, no, no. Not today. Please. I beg of you."

POUN-cer!

POUN-cer!

POUN-cer!

Miss Finch dropped her face into her hand. "You are killing me," she muttered . . . and noticed her TAs had fled to a safe distance.

Cowards.

POUNCER! POUNCER! POUNCER!

Foot stomping accompanied the demand.

POUNCER! POUNCER! POUNCER!

Miss Finch raised both hands, signaling her capitulation, and called out, "I surrender! A little decorum, if you please." She clambered down from her stool, unlatched the pet carrier, and stepped to her left several feet, then faced the carrier's door.

"Hugo, come."

What looked like a toy-sized Airedale but was actually a Welsh terrier popped out of the carrier. He circled Miss Finch three times, then sat directly in front of her, bright-eyed and attentive, his tongue lolling out one side of his mouth.

"Good boy, Hugo." She pulled a treat from her pocket and offered it to him.

Her class applauded and thundered, "Hu-GO! Hu-GO! Hu-GO!"

Miss Finch turned to her class. "Quiet, please. We do *not* wish to agitate her majesty, do we?"

Her TAs shook their heads, and a long, sighing "nooooo" from many of the students answered her.

Now facing the auditorium, her right side toward the pet carrier, and with Hugo sitting quite still, she called, "Pouncer, come."

A blur of creamy white fur, tipped in black, bounded from the carrier. It leaped upon Hugo's back and springboarded onto Miss Finch's shoulder. The cat perched there, her brilliant blue eyes glittering, basking in the room's complete and full attention, as was—in her world—her due.

"*POUN-cer! POUN-cer! POUN-cer!*"

Pouncer rubbed her jowls against Miss Finch's cheek and purred. Miss Finch smiled. She walked a few feet toward the seating, intending to say something.

However, at her approach, her TAs scattered. Those in the nearby front rows followed suit. One student opted to clamber over his seat back, where he promptly fell into the lap of a startled coed.

The rest of the hall chanted, "*POUN-cer! POUN-cer! POUN-cer!*"

Miss Finch walked the width of the auditorium's seating, giving her students a good look at Pouncer . . . or was she giving Pouncer a good look at her students?

"That is quite enough excitement for the present. Down, Pouncer," Miss Finch commanded.

Pouncer immediately "dethroned" herself onto Hugo's back, landed on the floor with a light *thump*, and marched with royal dignity into the carrier.

"You are a wonderful boy, Hugo," Miss Finch whispered. "Well done."

He turned and followed Pouncer.

"Now, may we *please* get on with this day's lesson?" Miss Finch asked. "Turn to Chapter 3, page seventy-nine."

———————•◆•———————

HER CLASS THAT day ended, as most of them did, with a flurry of raised hands and shouts of "Miss Finch! Miss Finch!" She pointed at a young man halfway up the tiered seats.

"Miss Finch, several of us have finished your book."

"Is that a question or are you angling for a gold star?" Titters and good-natured ribbing followed.

"No star necessary, thank you, but we, well, we've noticed striking similarities among your first four case studies."

"Have you? My, what a coincidence."

"But that's my point. We don't think they *are* co—"

"Next question."

She fielded three more questions in the same manner: brisk, no-nonsense, rapid-fire responses.

"That's all for today. We'll discuss Chapter 4 on Friday."

She picked up her briefcase—and hung on with a death grip when Miss Zhong attempted to abscond with it. She then grabbed the handle of her pet carrier and moved toward the door. Her TAs closed around her like a phalanx of self-appointed agents of the Secret Service.

The President should be so blessed, she scowled to herself.

In the lobby, two strangers spotted her and approached. The men were large and heavily muscled, their legs like bulging tree trunks. Their suits strained conspicuously across the breadth of their shoulders.

Miss Finch swallowed. *Bonafide enforcers. Why, these goons make Mr. Glenn look like junior varsity.*

"Need a word with you, Miss Finch," one of the men rumbled.

"Back off, kiddies," the other man ordered.

Shamefaced, her TAs hastened to do as they were told.

"Don Ettore Massimo has a message for you, lady."

She answered, her voice small, "Does he, indeed?"

"Yeah, *really* indeed. Don Massimo says you should pull your book from the market. In fact, he insists that you pull it from the market *and* issue a retraction, a public apology for your shoddy investigative work and for misleading the public to arrive at false conclusions."

Miss Finch's spit had completely dried up, but she managed to ask, "And why would I do that?"

"Well, because it would be a shame if you or, say, *your precious pets* met with, you know, an unfortunate *accident*."

The emphasis on the last word was impossible to miss, the meaning impossible to mistake—particularly in view of the fact that her book's underlying purpose was to expose six mob-ordered homicides disguised as ordinary, unremarkable traffic accidents.

All of them planned and executed by Antony Massimo, Don Massimo's only son.

"You've got forty-eight hours to convey the recall to your publisher and issue your apology. Do you understand Don Massimo's message?"

"Oh, I understand," she ground out.

The goons pivoted and lumbered toward an exit.

Her TAs returned. Not one of them would look her in the eye.

Miss Finch sighed. "Calling upon an oft-quoted nugget of Shakespearean wisdom, my friends, *discretion is the better part of valor.* I thank you for your concern, but you were no match for them. You were wise to accede to their demands."

"But w-w-who were they?" asked Mr. Donegal.

"Bad news, I'm afraid," she replied. In a softer voice, more to herself, she added, "Although I have been anticipating the arrival of such 'news.'"

Straightening her spine, she stated with all the confidence she could muster, "I will see you for class Friday," and marched toward the door.

They didn't take her brush-off well. Mr. Glenn spoke for the three of them as they fell in around her. "And we'll see you to your car, Miss Finch."

She nodded. "I thank you."

ONCE SHE WAS safely ensconced in her Range Rover with Hugo and Pouncer strapped into their padded harnesses on the SUV's backseat, Miss Finch picked up her phone, found a number in her contacts, pressed the dial icon, and set the phone in its car cradle. The phone rang, and the audio connected to her vehicle's speakers. She was backing out of her parking slot when someone answered her call.

"Gibson Security Services. How may I help you?"

"Miss BD Finch here. I have an order in place and would like to activate it."

"Of course, Miss Finch. One moment while I pull up your file. Ah. Here it is. You have requested two armed personal security specialists and 24-hour protection. We can activate that order within the hour. Will that work for you?"

"Yes. They may join me at my home."

"We'll send our people your way shortly."

"Pardon, but as a reminder, I hold a nondisclosure agreement signed by your CEO. All personnel assigned to guard me are bound by that agreement."

"You are correct, Miss Finch. I will stress that point with your detail."

———— • ————

HER DAY SHIFT guards, Grayson and Alberto, looked to be in their fifties and carried themselves like ex-military—probably because they were. She approved of them immediately.

"I picked up lunch for the three of us, then we're off to my afternoon tasks."

"Lunch for us? Thanks, Miss Finch," Grayson answered.

"Ditto. Where are we off to, Miss Finch?" Alberto asked.

"I own a small warehouse where I'm doing some refurbishments. Sort of a hobby of mine. That said, per my NDA with your company, the location of my warehouse is confidential information and is to remain so."

"Yes, ma'am. You can count on our discretion. We'll follow you there in our vehicle—after we sweep your house and your SUV for bugs and trackers."

Miss Finch's mouth formed a small "o." She whispered, "You are quite right, of course."

The man named Alberto pulled a hard-shelled case from the back of their vehicle, opened it, and the two men went to work. When they were done, they produced a single item to show her.

"This here," Grayson said, "is a tracker. Found it in the rear driver's side wheel well. From now on, we'll be sweeping your home and SUV any and every time they are left unattended."

Alberto dropped the tracker on Miss Finch's driveway. It produced a satisfying *crunch* as he drove his heel into it.

Miss Finch nodded. "Thank you."

"Hey, it's what we do and what you pay us for. We're ready to leave now if you are and will sweep the house when we return from your outing."

When they pulled up to the warehouse's perimeter, her guards insisted on taking her key, unlocking the gated fence and the warehouse doors, then clearing the building before they escorted her inside.

"Wow, Miss Finch," Grayson muttered. "You own a panel wagon? I've never seen a Ford Custom Country Squire in such great condition. What year is it?"

"1951. I have some finishing touches to add, but it's coming along nicely."

"I'll say!"

Alberto was more interested in her other project. "Your trailer looks like an old Casita. You gutted this thing? Took it down to its frame?"

"That 'thing,' had the misfortune of being used as a small meth lab by the ne'er-do-well son of a friend."

"Kid blew it up?"

"No, thank the Lord, otherwise neither he nor the trailer would have survived. His meth lab caught the trailer on fire, but he escaped with his life. I bought the ruined trailer, stripped it down, and am refurbishing it, plus certain customizations."

Alberto nodded. "Almost done, by the looks of it. Loving the coordinated paint job between the car and the trailer, by the way. That smoky blue and gray is quite striking."

"Thank you. I chose the color scheme and designed the detail work myself."

"Nice! What still needs work?"

"Among other things, I need to finish replumbing the bathroom and the kitchen sink."

"Want some help?"

She appraised him. "I hired you as security. How can you do your job if you are helping me?"

"From what we saw when we arrived, you have a chain-link perimeter fence with only one way in. Either Grayson or I can keep watch while the other one helps out. We can swap off every couple hours—unless you prefer we both keep watch."

"I agree that I'm fairly safe here and that only one of you needs to stand watch. Also, frankly, I would welcome the help. I believe I'm . . . on the clock, so to speak, to complete these projects."

Grayson frowned. "What exactly did you do to get on the bad side of the Lucchese Family?"

She shrugged. "I authored a book that has drawn wide attention to a number of traffic fatalities. Let's just say once the various police departments of the case studies I present in the book reexamine those cases, their revised conclusions won't reflect well on Don Massimo or his associates."

Grayson and Alberto exchanged concerned looks. Grayson blurted, "Lady, are you suicidal?"

"Suicidal? Some might say I am, but if I *were*, why would I bother with you?"

Alberto laughed. "Good point." He tipped his head toward her trailer. "I can help you with the plumbing."

"Your assistance would be much appreciated. I'm installing a tankless water heater next. I'm a fair plumber, but would appreciate a second set of eyes while I wire the water heater's electrical and add the liquid propane connections.

"But first?" She tipped her chin at the bag she carried. "Let us enjoy a spot of lunch, shall we?"

FINCH INVESTIGATIONS

CHAPTER 2

MISS FINCH ARRIVED at her Friday class in Grayson and Alberto's vehicle and in their company. Her overprotective TAs took one look at the implacable expressions of the career soldiers flanking her and, metaphorically, bared their bellies.

"Oh, you can trust my teaching assistants," Miss Finch told Grayson and Alberto in her TAs' hearing. "They are loyal to a fault."

Glenn, Donegal, and Zhong beamed. Miss Zhong added, "I'm glad to see you have *real* bodyguards now. Those . . . men in suits were scary."

Grayson interrupted. "Men in suits?"

"They delivered a message to me, courtesy of Don Massimo."

"They threatened you? Here? In public? To your face?"

"Threatened me and my darlings." She gestured to her pet carrier.

Grayson was not happy. "You told our boss you needed protection from the Lucchese family, but you didn't say their goons had actually threatened you. We need to know these things!"

"It only happened day before yesterday," Miss Finch murmured. "I had been waiting to activate my request for protection until I felt the need."

He scowled. "Yeah? Well, 'I feel the need' is generally *preceded* by the impact of a bullet—too late for us to do a blessed thing about it! From here on out, please do not withhold pertinent info from us."

His eyes swept the lobby. "As soon as we settle you in your classroom, I will reconnoiter this building while Alberto remains with you."

Her guards walked her into the auditorium and blanched at the size of the crowd.

"*This* is your classroom?" Alberto demanded. "You didn't say it was the size of a small concert hall!"

Grayson's unhappiness quotient shot up another notch. "Yeah, with seating for about five hundred possible threats?"

Miss Finch dismissed his concern with a wave of her hand. "Don't fret over my students. I doubt the mob would send a fresh-faced scholar to take me out."

"We're more like her f-f-fan club," Mr. Donegal said. "Half of this crowd isn't even enrolled in h-her class, but they've bought and are reading her book."

"Fan club?" Mr. Glenn snorted. "More like the newest cult favorite. Until the mysteries buried in your book are fully dissected and understood, I don't foresee your popularity waning."

"I hear s-s-seventeen s-s-study groups have formed to discuss it," Donegal added.

Miss Finch's brows disappeared into the curly, silver-shot wisps on her forehead. "Seventeen study groups? Merciful heavens! No wonder there's standing room only this morning."

Zhong shrugged. "Not every day we get to see history in the making."

"Oh dear."

"Your assassination won't be part of that history," Alberto hastened to promise her.

"And yet somehow your assurances are not all that comforting."

———— ● ————

MONDAY, WINTER QUARTER, WEEK FIVE

THE NEXT TWO weeks passed uneventfully. Monday through Friday, 6:00 a.m. through 6:00 p.m. Grayson and Alberto accompanied Miss Finch wherever she went, primarily to teach her class or to work on her restorations. At shift change, Addie and Dorian took over. Miss Finch shared her weekends with yet another four guards, who relieved her weekly protective detail.

"Miss Finch, I have a question," Grayson murmured, as they pulled up to the warehouse.

"I cannot promise you an answer," she replied, "but I can promise to listen."

He snarked, "That sounds just like you, playing your cards close to the vest. My question is, what are your plans for this car and this . . . travel trailer? And why all the secrecy?"

"You have asked two questions, Grayson."

"May I have an answer to both?"

She chuckled. "I appreciate your unfailing civility, and since you and Alberto both possess a high degree of deductive reasoning, I may be able to answer both questions in a single word: *contingencies*."

Grayson and Alberto sighed in concert, and Grayson said, "*This* is your bugout plan? Seriously?"

"God willing, and I am still alive to use such a plan."

Alberto frowned. "You don't think we can keep you safe?"

"I think you increase the odds that I'll live to see my next birthday—April, by the way—but nothing is set in stone."

Alberto, still frowning, said, "I'm not feeling the love, are you, Grayson?"

"Nope. I'm offended."

"It is neither a matter of love nor of competence, gentlemen. If the Lucchese Family wants me dead, they will find a way. On the other hand, I trust God to thwart them."

"Still offended," Grayson muttered.

Alberto looked thoughtful. "Didn't take you for a religious person."

"Goodness, I hope I am not! I *am*, however, a follower of Jesus."

"There's a difference?"

"I believe there is. By and large, religious people learn and follow rules and rituals. Christians—Bible-believing Christians, that is—learn and follow Jesus."

"Interesting. And you think he'll keep you safe?"

"He has his ways. Why, I even think you two are part of his SOP."

"You don't say."

"Oh, but I do say."

"*Fine*. Well, just so you know, we haven't seen any indication that you are being followed, harassed, or threatened—not since we removed that tracking device—and Gibson Security is keeping one eye on the Lucchese Family, Don Massimo in particular. We also know the Family's enforcers by name, and we sweep your car and home several times a day."

"Ah, but do you check my phone calls? Business dealings? Publishing status? My attorneys?"

Grayson cut in. "What aren't you telling us?"

"Quite a lot, in point of fact. Do you, for example, know that I am a licensed PI and the sole owner-operator of Finch Investigations?"

Grayson gaped. "You're a *what?*"

"A mere hobbyist, I assure you, but shall we return to what is happening behind the scenes that you are, apparently, blind to? After threatening me and my little darlings personally if I didn't pull my book from the market—and me ignoring them—the mob then threatened my publisher. When my publisher's lawyers tried to pull my book over my objections, *my* attorneys slapped them down for breach of contract."

She took a deep breath. "And I have connections in the world of private investigations, gentlemen. For the most part, I find out what's happening before it actually occurs. For example, shortly—as soon as tomorrow—a prominent LA businessman will hold a press conference to announce that my book has smeared his reputation, thus he is suing me for libel. My proactive attorneys are all over that too.

"Of course, the next step in this disagreeable little parade will be a bounty on yours truly, followed by some sort of direct attack. At that point, I do hope you earn your keep—I truly do. And since the California branch of the Lucchese Family does nothing without Don Massimo's specific knowledge and approval, each of these actions must, therefore, *originate* with Don Massimo.

"Lastly, contrary to your assertions, I would say the attacks I have just rehearsed are the very definition of harassment and threats. Now do you understand why I cannot lean all of my confidence on you, as competent as you both are? If I am to survive, I must have more in my arsenal than just you. And for your information, I lean on the Lord to guide me in all my preparations."

She pushed a wisp of hair out of her eyes and exhaled slowly. "For example, I have taken note of Winston Churchill's brilliant insights. While the world was fretting over Hitler, Churchill spotted another adversary on the horizon: *Russia*. Churchill called Russia 'a riddle, wrapped in a mystery, inside an enigma,' a profound puzzle that confused and stymied the West's best intelligence efforts for a time. I have determined to make myself as much like Russia as possible: a profound puzzle and a perplexing conundrum to my enemies."

Alberto nodded slowly. "Uh, so far? I think you're killing it."

Grayson snarled, "Killing it? Great choice of words, 'Berto."

"Sorry," Alberto muttered.

"Now, now, children. Let us play nice."

Grayson stared at his feet. "Yeah. What he said. Still . . ."

Miss Finch went on. "Still, to accomplish my little feat of survival, secrets and contingency plans are needful. Vital, even."

Grayson gnawed his lower lip. Alberto, hands on his hips, walked several feet away, swore under his breath, then walked back.

"What can we do to help you other than what we're doing, Miss Finch?"

She smiled and gently patted his arm. "We all have a part to play in the theater of my continued existence. To date, you are playing your part well, both of you. I only hope that, when the time comes and I truly need your help, you will answer my call."

Grayson said, "Whatever you need, Miss Finch."

Alberto nodded his agreement. "We won't fail you."

"Thank you. I appreciate you more than you know, but sadly . . . all of us fail at some point."

She looked aside then. "Only God never fails."

———— ● ————

GRAYSON AND ALBERTO accompanied Miss Finch back home, arriving before their 6:00 p.m. shift change. Addie and Dorian were waiting to relieve them, but their serious-as-a-heart-attack expressions set Miss Finch's teeth on edge.

Grayson responded first. "What's happened?"

Addie slid her eyes toward Miss Finch, then back. "Mail came. We went to collect it and found a gift box that did not arrive via USPS and was apparently left on the walk next to the mail box. We took the precaution of scanning the unopened box before examining its contents."

"Where is it?"

"We left the box and regular mail on Miss Finch's desk."

"No explosives or other dangerous residue?"

"Nope. We checked the contents thoroughly."

"And?"

"And while not exactly a horse's severed head, the message is just as pointed."

Grayson and Alberto strode toward the house ahead of Miss Finch; Addie and Dorian waited and watched Miss Finch's back while she removed Hugo and Pouncer from her Range Rover, then followed her into the house. The five of them converged on Miss Finch's office.

Grayson had already lifted the lid on the colorful box and was staring inside. His jaw was clenched so tight it flexed under the pressure.

"Show me," Miss Finch demanded.

He moved aside. She took his place. Looked inside.

As her conscious mind processed the contents, her body "got it" and reacted first. Nausea roiled in her gut. She swallowed several times, trying to keep her stomach's contents in their proper place.

In the box were two stuffed animals, a small white cat and a small black-and-gray dog.

Both animals had been decapitated, their heads ripped off. Red-tinted stuffing hung from the detached heads in ghastly ribbons.

Alberto grabbed a nearby waste can and thrust it under Miss Finch's chin just in time. Even while heaving into the can, several thoughts ran through her head.

Lord, I trust you. I may fail you, I may soon suffer and die, but with all my heart I believe what I told Grayson and Alberto.

You never fail.

CHAPTER 3

THE PREDICTED ATTACK came out of left field and from a source she least expected.

Grayson and Alberto had followed Miss Finch in their vehicle to a downtown restaurant where she was to join a birthday party luncheon for her friend Dinah. Before they left for the party, Grayson gave her the operational rundown.

"Alberto will clear the restaurant before you go inside. He will then enjoy a nice lunch at a table near you where he can monitor for threats while I watch over your vehicle and eat a tepid Cup O' Noodles."

"Tough job, but somebody's got to do it," Alberto snarked.

Miss Finch cocked an eyebrow at Grayson. "I take it Alberto prevailed at Rock, Paper, Scissors?"

"Whatever. When the lunch ends and you are ready to leave, give 'Berto a sign."

"Got it."

She parked, retrieved Hugo and Pouncer from her back seat, and placed them in their carrier. Under Grayson and Alberto's watchful eyes, she entered the restaurant, pulling the carrier behind her, her mind on the festivities ahead. The celebration was not only for Dinah's birthday but also for her retirement from her career with the US Post Office.

Five unmarried career women—women Miss Finch had known for decades—were already gathered around a festively decorated table. Miss Finch joined the party and parked Hugo and Pouncer's carrier beside her chair. The women ordered, ate together, caught up on each other's lives, and laughed often.

Later, as they indulged in dessert, Dinah went around the table and asked each of them when they intended to retire and what their plans might be. Miss Finch was last.

"BD, what are your retirement plans?" Dinah asked. "And isn't your birthday in April?"

"It is, but since I'll only be sixty-two, I have a few years to decide when and how to take the leap." She added thoughtfully, "Frankly, I'm enjoying my stint at UCLA as a guest lecturer, I have another book in the works, and I still dabble in my PI business. Goodness! At present, I don't think I have *time* to retire!"

Her friends had a good laugh, and Melanie shook her head. "You have had the most interesting life of us all, BeeDee. Why, the stories we've heard you tell! Peace Corps, volunteer here, volunteer there, amateur this, professional that, now a licensed private detective? I was a civil engineer with the same company for forty years. Talk about *boring*."

Dinah smiled at Melanie. "Not as boring as forty years spent as a government bureaucrat. We can't all be like BD—she's pretty much one of a kind. Why, just listening to her tell of her exploits raises my blood pressure!"

"Absolutely!" Gretchen agreed. "The 'adventures' I have planned for my retirement are tame in comparison to pretty much everything she's done and continues to do."

Miss Finch blushed. "And here I thought this was *your* celebration, Dinah. Speaking of which . . ." She produced a small wrapped gift and passed it across the table. "Happy birthday, dear friend."

"But I said no gifts!"

"And *I* said *hogwash*."

"So did I!" Betty laughed.

"And I," Laurel, Gretchen, and Melanie chimed in.

Accompanied by more laughter, five gifts appeared in front of Dinah's dish of melting ice cream. The hilarity from their table made nearby guests look up and grin.

"You are the best friends ever," Dinah sniffed.

"To the best friends ever," Miss Finch said, raising her iced tea.

"Hear, hear!"

When the party began to break up, Miss Finch texted Dinah, asking if she would mind staying behind for a moment. When only the two of them were left at the table, Miss Finch moved to the chair beside Dinah's.

"I wanted to update you in person," she said quietly.

"I am praying daily for you, BD."

"Thank you—my team and I greatly appreciate your prayers."

"Your team? What does that mean?"

Miss Finch nodded. "I have hired a personal protection team. One of them is here in the restaurant; the other is outside, keeping watch on my vehicle."

"That is a wise move, BD. You know what would be even wiser?"

Miss Finch sighed. "Please do not start with me."

"I am your friend, BD. I wish I understood why you're bent on putting yourself in danger."

"I will tell you when all is done, Dinah. In the meantime, I wanted to let you know that my 'bugout' plan, as my security team calls it, is nearly ready to implement. God willing, I intend to finish out the quarter at UCLA next month, then sneak out of town and live on the road the next few months, never staying long in any one place, basically spending the summer where I will be personally unknown and my presence fairly anonymous."

"How will you manage the anonymous part?"

"You know that burner phone I call and text you on?"

Dinah nodded.

"I would never knowingly embroil you in my plans, Dinah, which is why I haven't called or texted you on my regular phone for the last six months and have asked you to do the same. After I disappear, I do not want Don Massimo's people showing up on your doorstep looking for me. That would not be good for you."

Dinah shivered a little. "No, indeed."

"Given today's technologies, I'm certain Don Massimo's people know exactly who I call or text on a regular basis. I am also convinced they are using my phone to monitor my whereabouts, which is why I will ditch my regular phone before I leave town. I have bought up half a dozen more burners to use and 'lose' as needed."

"You're telling me this in case you call and I don't recognize the number."

"Yes. Those extra phones are with me wherever I go. Just in case."

They hugged as they parted.

"God be with you, BD."

"And with you, my dear friend."

Minutes later, Miss Finch left the restaurant, nodding to Alberto on her way out. She loaded Hugo and Pouncer into her SUV, backed out of her parking slot, and drove in the direction of her warehouse. Grayson and Alberto followed close behind her.

———————— • ————————

ABOUT TWO MILES from her warehouse, Miss Finch exited the elevated freeway into a commercial area. She'd found that taking surface streets the rest of the way to the warehouse beat the freeway's congestion. She hummed to herself, recalling Dinah's birthday lunch, and thanking God for the many friends she'd made through the years.

A red light stopped her at a congested intersection. As Miss Finch waited, she glanced to her right at the elevated freeway that ran parallel to the road she was on. She found Grayson and Alberto's gray 4x4 in her rearview mirror, two vehicles back, and was gratified at their near presence.

Strident honking pulled her from her thoughts. The light she'd stopped for was still red, and cross-street traffic was moving, but the honking of horns, mainly on her left, increased in number and volume.

Then she saw it: A tanker truck crossing the intersection from her left had abruptly changed lanes—no, *had cut across two lanes*—causing frantic reactions. Tires screeched, horns blared, and cars and trucks rear-ended vehicles that braked sharply to avoid being hit by the tanker truck.

Miss Finch's mouth opened. *That tanker. It is coming for me.*

The horror unfolded in slow motion.

Miss Finch floored the Range Rover, choosing to risk traffic crossing from the right rather than being crushed by the oncoming tanker on her left. But in an excruciatingly slow and prolonged timelapse, she was hardly beyond the crosswalks and into the intersection when she realized she would not escape: She was going to be T-boned by forty tons of accelerating machinery—and there was not a blessed thing she could do to prevent it.

The truck bore down on her. Instinctively, as if to ward off her imminent death, she put up her left hand and cried out, "Lord Jesus! Please save me!"

The near corner of the tanker's cab struck her vehicle. Her door caved. The SUV's frame buckled. She screamed in agony. The pain was so all-encompassing, so overwhelming, she could not even tell where it came from, but she knew it would be short-lived.

Because I will be under the tanker's wheels.

Dead.

Oh, Lord Jesus!

The tanker's cab loomed above her, the face of the driver larger than life . . . and getting even larger. No! The driver was crashing through his windshield!

She watched in stunned horror as the body of *Antony Massimo* shredded its way through the tanker's windshield and landed, bloody and broken, across the hood and windshield of her Range Rover.

But the tanker's cab—instead of rolling over her car and crushing her—seemed to *bounce back* from the impact.

What?

Did you do that, Lord? Did you just put your hand between me and that tanker to save me from being flattened under its wheels?

Before her incredulity could even register, her Range Rover shot forward like a pit squeezed from a cherry into the center of the intersection, where it spun wildly, pitching her round and round like a rock in a tumbler despite her seatbelt. While being spun and tumbled like wet clothes in a dryer, the broken body of Tony Massimo slid first one way, then another across her hood, and she was amazed it did not fly off her vehicle altogether.

She was also convinced that, while spinning, she had caught a glimpse of the tanker's trailer swinging wide, breaking free from the cab, and continuing on, sideways, across the intersection. In that instant, an odd thought flashed through her mind.

I do hope the liquid in that tanker's load is nothing flammable.

Her car finished tossing her round and round and shuddered to a stop. She couldn't move. Her neck felt frozen, and it prevented her from moving her head to look around her. She could not even turn away from the dreadful sight of Tony Massimo's body sprawled right there in front of her face, only the bloody, crazed glass of her windshield between them.

Time stood still until, jarring her further, she heard a horrendous, screeching crash behind and off to her right. The horrible sounds worried her, but she could not shift her position to see what had happened. Even when she tried to recall what was to the right of the intersection where she'd been waiting for the light to change, only the image of the elevated freeway rose before her.

Could the tanker's trailer have collided with the underpinnings of the overpass?

Her speculations were overturned by a fearsome and fiery explosion. Her hands flew to her face to shield her eyes from the intensity of the heat. That was when the pain from her trapped ankle finally found its voice. It screamed. It shrieked. It struck her with the force of an avalanche, shock, distress, and agony vying for dominance.

The pain was too much!

Too much! Too much! Too much!

Somewhere inside, she gave up.

Take me home now, Lord God. Please. I cannot stand it!

No, wait—Hugo and Pouncer! Please save them. Find them good homes together . . .

A panicked voice cut through her mental fog. "Miss Finch! Miss Finch!"

Grayson?

"Open your eyes, Miss Finch."

I can't. The pain, the pain, the pain. My ankle is on fire!

"Hold on, Miss Finch. Help is coming."

Slowly, she drew a breath and moved her lips. "M-my darlings . . ."

"Hugo and Pouncer are all right, shaken but okay. Don't worry. We'll take care of them. Please, trust us. We'll take care of everything."

CHAPTER 4

SHE BECAME AWARE of bright lights and throbbing pain. Unbearable pain. Without meaning to, she moaned.

"Miss Finch? I'm Dr. Stratford. You've been in an accident and are in a hospital emergency department. Can you open your eyes?"

The light hurt her eyes, but she opened them anyway, only to squint under the white glare.

"Miss Finch, you have numerous abrasions, strains, and bruises, and your ankle is severely broken. It requires immediate surgery. We have permission paperwork for the surgery ready for you to sign. Are you able to sign or is there someone here authorized to sign for you?"

A voice somewhere behind the doctor spoke. "I'm the lead on Miss Finch's protective detail. If she provides verbal permission, I will sign for her."

Grayson.

"Yes," she muttered. "He can . . . sign."

"Nurse, please witness the signature and note Miss Finch's verbal permission for this gentleman to provide it."

"Will do, Doctor."

"Good. Now, Miss Finch, we're going to put you under. Here we go; just rest. We'll take good care of . . ."

———— ● ————

WHEN SHE NEXT came awake, the overhead lights were dim, and she lay in a bed closely surrounded by curtains. She tried to turn her head; it hurt too much. She moaned and blinked her eyes. Something rustled off to the side. A face loomed over her.

"Miss Finch? It's Alberto. The surgery is over, and you're in recovery."

She tested her voice. It was rough, her throat sore.

A straw touched her lips, and she pulled it eagerly into her mouth. The cold water that hit the back of her raw throat had never felt or tasted so good.

"My darlings . . ."

"Grayson has them, but I think he's afraid to let Pouncer out for a potty break. We took everything from your Range Rover that was loose, including your phone. Do you want me to call anyone for you?"

"No. Need pet carrier."

"Like I said, Grayson has Hugo and Pouncer."

She shook her head. "In the carrier . . . under my darlings' bed."

Alberto got on his phone. "Gray, yeah, listen, Miss Finch says to look under the pet carrier's mattress. She wants whatever's in there. No, I don't know what to do about Pouncer. Well, I'm not touching her either!"

Miss Finch reached for his arm. "Wait. Bring them to me when . . . I'm in my room."

Alberto spoke into his phone again. "Miss Finch says bring Hugo and Pouncer to her as soon as she's in her room. Yeah, I'm right there with you—I'd choose the risk of sneaking Hugo and Pouncer into Miss Finch's room over Pouncer shredding the mess outta me. Okay, I'll let you know when they move her to a room."

———◆———

MISS FINCH DOZED on and off until they rolled her recovery bed into a semi-private room and transferred her to the bed closest to the window. The second bed in the room was, as yet, unoccupied. She was in nearly unbearable pain until her nurse set up a morphine drip.

"Doctor's orders. We'll keep you on the drip for the next twenty-four hours, then step you down to pills. And we need to keep you here at least a couple of days—monitor you for other injuries and help you get ahead of the pain so you can manage it. Guess they had to cut you out of the wreckage, and your ankle, to be frank, was crushed when the door of your vehicle was hit. According to your chart, you are now the proud 'forever home' of the plate and pins the surgical team used to put the pieces back together. I'll be by later to check on you."

"Thank you." She suddenly recalled the empty eyes of Tony Massimo staring at her through the bloody, broken glass of her windshield.

"Alberto?"

"Here, Miss Finch."

"The driver of the tanker truck . . ."

"Guess he didn't make it."

"I know. Saw him . . . on hood of Range Rover. Massimo."

"Don Massimo? You think he ordered the hit?"

She automatically tried to shake her head, but the pain forced a groan from her.

"Hey, Miss Finch, you're going to be pretty sore for a while—neck and back plus bruises galore. Nasty cut on your left arm."

She turned inward. Fixed her mind on locating her left arm. It felt numb and out of touch.

She gestured with her right hand for Alberto to come closer. "Driver."

He leaned over her so she could see him. "You recognized the driver?"

"Antony . . . Massimo."

"What! You're sure?"

Considering his dead face was plastered all over my windshield? Yes, I'm sure! Huh. I see my sense of cruel irony escaped unscathed.

"Yes."

"You think his father ordered the hit?"

"No."

The morphine drip machine hummed briefly, and she sighed with relief.

"You're saying Tony Massimo took the hit upon himself because you fingered him for the 'accident' case studies in your book?"

"Yes, but Don Massimo will . . . will . . ."

She couldn't find the right word, and the world, although slowly drifting farther away, was rosier than it had been, the pain greatly diminished.

Oh. The morphine. Well . . . shoot.

"You think the Don will blame you?"

Her mouth wasn't working right. Couldn't find her tongue either. "Yesh . . ."

"You should rest now, Miss Finch."

Like I have any control over that . . .

SHE WOKE WITH a start, filled with dread. "Alberto!"

"I'm here; you're safe."

She immediately calmed.

"And Grayson?"

"On his way."

"Have him bring up Hugo and Pouncer, please."

"Will do. Also . . ."

Miss Finch managed to turn her face to him. "Yes?"

"We have you fully covered, Miss Finch. Addie is in the hall just outside your door, and Dorian is hanging out at the elevator with a sightline to the stairs at the other end. At least two of us will be here, one on your door at all times, until you're released. *No one* is getting past us."

She nodded, relieved, but already deep in her contingency plans. "Need you to pull the SIM card from my phone. Snap it."

"What about your contacts?"

"Stored in the cloud."

"Good."

———— ⬦ ————

THIRTY MINUTES LATER, Grayson arrived, pulling the pet carrier behind him, his windbreaker casually draped over it.

"Told the nurses it was your suitcase," he whispered.

"Well done. Hugo?"

"Took him for a walk in a nearby park; managed to keep Pouncer from jetting out of the carrier or, alternatively, attaching herself to my face."

"Set the carrier on the chair and open it, please."

"Uh, you sure?"

"I suppose we should close the door to the hallway. Oh, and open the bathroom door. Wide open, please."

After Alberto did so, Grayson unlatched the pet carrier.

"Hugo, come."

Hugo poked his nose out, saw her, barked once, then leaped up on the bed. He nosed her and snuggled into her arms.

"Pouncer? Come."

Pouncer peered cautiously from the carrier. She yowled plaintively.

"I know, I know," Miss Finch said softly. "Come to Mama."

Pouncer made the leap and immediately nuzzled Miss Finch's face, yowling intermittently.

"Yes, I know. Bathroom, Pouncer. Bathroom!"

When Pouncer sprang from the bed, Grayson and Alberto sprang too. Grayson flattened himself against a wall; Alberto dragged a chair between himself and Pouncer.

Pouncer ignored them both. She padded quickly around the room, found the open door, and disappeared inside.

"What's she doing?" Grayson asked in a whisper.

"Using the toilet."

He looked from her to Alberto, then back. "No way."

The toilet in the bathroom flushed.

"Way," Miss Finch snickered. "Now, please pull the pet bed from the carrier. You'll see it's actually two beds, one atop the other, the bottom bed hollowed out and a fake floor added. Bring me one of the burner phones you find under the bottom bed's fake floor. I have calls to make."

Once she'd set up the phone Grayson retrieved for her and downloaded her contacts from one of her cloud accounts, she sent both of her guards from the room. Hugo was dozing on her right side, Pouncer snuggled up against her head as if perched on her shoulder, when she made her first call.

"Dinah? BD here. Yes, it was a lovely party indeed. Me? Oh, I suppose I've been better. Do you recall that distasteful ditty, *Grandma Got Run Over by a Reindeer?* I can now relate. Someone tried to run us over with a tanker truck."

She listened until Dinah began to recover from her shock, and her anxious rush of words slowed. "Injuries? A number. My neck is quite sore, I have a few cuts and bruises, and I suppose the worst of it is my ankle. The truck caved in my door and . . . crushed it."

She answered Dinah's questions until she realized her head was pounding frightfully. "Dinah, listen, I'm going to need your help sooner than I anticipated, and given my present condition, we have new details to iron out. Yes, thank you."

They spoke at length before they concluded to Miss Finch's satisfaction. She rubbed her eyes, tried to stretch her inflamed neck, then found the three numbers she needed and placed her next call.

"Mr. Glenn, Miss Finch here. Yes, I have a new number. I apologize for calling so late, but I have a situation. Would you allow me to conference in Miss Zhong and Mr. Donegal before I go over it? Thank you."

When her three TAs were on the line, she related the barest of details around her "accident."

When their words of outrage and concern tapered off, she said, "Since I cannot get up and around just yet, I need the three of you to cover my lecture tomorrow."

Into the babble of their shocked objections, she injected, "Look here, even if all you do is read aloud from my book, you can and *must* handle the lecture tomorrow. Just, whatever you do, do not allow the Q&A to devolve into speculation—or better yet, skip the Q&A."

"When do you—"

"No, Miss Zhong, I have no idea when I will be back." She began thinking aloud. "Perhaps the university can arrange for a substitute. The dean may even insist upon it."

Mr. Glenn objected immediately. "No one could possibly sub for you, Miss Finch—it's *your* course based on *your* book! The three of us will be lucky to get through your class tomorrow without your students and the class lurkers lynching us."

Miss Zhong added, "We'll have to play on their sympathies for you just to get away with it this one time."

"Agree," Mr. Donegal said.

"Me too," added Mr. Glenn.

Miss Finch sighed. "You are probably right. I suppose if I am up to it, I could videoconference in and teach the class that way, but not yet. Not tomorrow."

Her TAs jabbered their approval of her idea until she cut them off. "All right, all right! I will videoconference in for as much of the remainder of the term as I can . . . although due to my circumstances, a sub may have to slog through one or two classes. With your joint assistance, of course."

An unwelcome thought hit her. *What if Don Massimo's goons show up at my class looking for information on my whereabouts? My eager-to-please but spineless TAs turned to jelly at the goons' previous visit. Should Massimo's enforcers return, they would certainly attempt to pump my TAs dry. Perhaps . . . yes, I should provide my little birdies with a pat, uniform answer.*

"Please listen carefully. Should those threatening, er, *gentlemen* visit my class again, I want you to tell them I am out for the remainder of the quarter. If they ask anything further, your response to each and every question *must* be 'We do not know.' You do not know where I am. You do not know the details of my injuries. You do not know where I am being treated. You do not know *anything*, including the university's disposition of my class. Is that understood?"

Mr. Glenn asked, "You want us to lie about your plans to teach your class by videoconference?"

"Considering that those *gentlemen* do not have my best interests at heart, I do, indeed, expect you to lie—and it had best be an Oscar-worthy performance. In fact, you are to tell the same tall tale to *any* stranger asking about me. After all, no one has the right to my personal business. Now, will you do it, just as I have told you? Can I expect you to follow my instructions to the letter?"

When she heard a unified "Yes, Miss Finch," she added, "Very good. Now, be aware that when I call you again, it may be from another unknown number, so do pick up my call."

Her baby birds chirped, "Yes, Miss Finch."

"Excellent. I thank you for your concern for my well-being, and I appreciate the three of you very much. Goodbye for now."

She hung up and lay back on her pillows, begging the shrieking pain in her neck to calm down. Keeping quite still seemed to help some, but . . .

"But I cannot keep still. Not if I hope to survive even another week."

She called Grayson. He and Alberto reappeared in minutes.

"What's up, Miss Finch?"

"My friend Dinah will be here inside an hour. She will take Hugo and Pouncer home with her."

"Can't say I'm not relieved," Grayson admitted. "Hugo's great, but I'm scared spitless of Pouncer."

Hearing her name, Pouncer's head came up. She fixed Grayson with her icy blue stare. He backed to a safe distance.

Miss Finch sniffed. "Any idea how long I'll be cooped up in this place?"

"Good grief! You just got here, Miss Finch. You have to give your body time to heal!" Alberto tried not to sound outraged . . . and failed.

"Am I reasonably safe here?"

"We think so—and your surgeon said you *need* to stay at least a couple of days. Get you stabilized and all."

A knock sounded at the door, and a nurse entered. She stopped, frowned, and addressed Grayson and Alberto. "Who are you? This patient is in no fit shape to receive visitors."

Grayson assumed his most professional demeanor. "I am the lead on Miss Finch's security detail. You can expect to see us and two additional members of Miss Finch's team throughout her stay. Furthermore, we will be monitoring every individual who comes through that door. We will not permit anyone without proper ID and a legitimate purpose to enter her room."

The nurse's brows lifted. "I see . . . I think."

She turned to Miss Finch. "Miss Finch, I'm Jackie, your meds nurse. From one to ten, what's your current pain—oh! What in heaven's name are these animals doing on your bed!"

"Comforting me, I assure you."

"No, no, no. You cannot have them here—this is *not* allowed."

Pouncer growled low in her throat and showed her teeth; Jackie, eyes wide, edged away.

"I am aware of hospital rules, Jackie-my-meds-nurse; however, my darlings were in the car with me when we were hit. We simply had to see and assure each other that we will be okay. I have made arrangements for them, and they should be gone within the hour. But you were asking about my pain?"

Jackie, keeping one eye on Pouncer, repeated, "From one to ten, what is your current pain level?"

"Oh, I'd say about half past 'nearly intolerable' verging on 'I'm about to gnaw my foot off to get some relief.'"

Behind Nurse Jackie, Alberto rolled his eyes.

Pouncer, attempting to intimidate Jackie further, growled again.

Jackie crab-walked to the foot of Miss Finch's bed—away from Pouncer—and edged cautiously up the opposite side. "I'm going to . . . up your morphine drip a touch."

"I thank you for your mercy! And when will my surgeon be by to visit me?"

"He came by after dinner, but I believe you were asleep. You probably won't see him until tomorrow after dinner."

Miss Finch blinked stupidly. "He came after dinner? Why, what time is it now?"

Jackie looked at her watch. "Oh, I'd say about half past nine, verging on bedtime."

Grayson snickered.

BD was about to send him a scathing reproof when her stomach lurched and rumbled so loudly, three sets of eyes jinked toward her. Even Pouncer looked startled.

"Perhaps I am a touch on the hungry side . . . having missed dinner."

Jackie gestured to a laminated sheet on the nightstand. "That is the patient menu. Call the number at the top, tell them what you'd like, and they will send it up to you—but do eat sparingly. Your system is recovering from the shock of injury followed by surgery, and the general anesthesia hasn't altogether left your system. We don't want you upchucking in your present condition—do we?"

Miss Finch's tight, pursed mouth was the only answer she got.

"I'll look in on you again around midnight. I hope to find you sleeping—without your, er, darlings."

No sooner had Jackie left than another knock sounded on the door. Alberto opened it a crack.

"Yes?"

"Hi, um, I'm Dinah, BD's friend?"

He glanced back at Miss Finch.

"Yes, that is Dinah."

Hugo jumped from the bed, ran up to Dinah, and sat. He looked up expectantly.

"Oh, dear—I'm so sorry, Hugo. I haven't any treats on me."

Grayson hissed under his breath. "Wow. I haven't given a single thought to feeding Hugo and Pouncer, Miss Finch. They must be starving and thirsty."

Dinah smiled. "Don't worry; I bought food for them on my way here. I'll take good care of your babies, BD."

"I know you will, Dinah. Thank you; you truly are a friend indeed." She motioned to Alberto. "Would you kindly place the carrier on the floor, door open?"

She called to Hugo. "Come, Hugo. Carrier."

Hugo trotted over and into the carrier.

"Pouncer, carrier."

Pouncer turned her face up to Miss Finch's and warbled a protest.

"I know, my darling, but they will not allow me to keep you here. Go with Hugo."

Pouncer sat up. Arched her back and stretched. She jumped down onto the floor, stuck her nose in the air, and pranced into the carrier.

Dinah latched the door, then drew near the bed. "I'm praying for you, BD." She glanced at Grayson and Alberto, then dropped her voice to a whisper. "I'll be making those arrangements tomorrow; we can leave any time after they are complete."

Miss Finch whispered back, "I probably shouldn't leave until I have my pain under control. They have me on a morphine drip at present."

Dinah nodded, her forehead wrinkled in concern. "Will those men be able to keep you safe while you're here?"

"How many guards did you pass on your way to my room?"

"Two, I think. The first, when I got off the elevator, the second, a very determined-looking young woman outside your door."

"You can stop whispering over there—we can hear every word," Grayson said. "And yes, we *will* keep her safe."

"You have my thanks," Dinah answered.

She turned back to Miss Finch. "I'll be awaiting your call."

Miss Finch wore a distracted expression. "You know, Dinah, the strangest thing happened when that truck hit me. I keep going over it in my mind, seeing the same incredible chain of events again and again," she said softly.

"You may not be recalling things accurately."

"I am aware of the phenomenon, which is why I have been rerunning my memory, but the scene is quite clear. I have come to the conclusion that the Lord spit my Range Rover out from under that truck and by doing so, preserved my life."

Grayson and Alberto drew near, and Dinah leaned in closer. "This I have got to hear!"

Miss Finch closed her eyes to visualize the details. "As the tanker's cab hit us, it was as though a giant hand stopped its forward momentum and momentarily pushed the cab backward."

Grayson muttered, "Pushed the cab backward?"

"Yes, the cab hit, then seemed to rebound—right after Antony Massimo made his, er, *passage* through his windshield and onto the Range Rover. At nearly the same time, that same hand shoved my Range Rover forward, out from under cab—because as soon as we were clear, the truck's trailer swung forward, broke loose from the cab, and kept right on going, skidding toward the freeway underpinnings."

"You must be misremembering," Grayson muttered. "That cab couldn't have stopped just like that."

"But you were there! Did you not see the tanker's trailer—*without the cab*—skid across the intersection, hit the overpass supports, and explode?"

"Of course, but that other thing? The cab hitting you, then bouncing back? Not possible," Alberto muttered, shaking his head.

Miss Finch's one-sided smile was wry. "And yet, had that *not* happened, the cab should have rolled over my Range Rover, and I would be dead."

Dinah blew out a long breath. "God is merciful!"

"Yes, he is—to him be all the glory."

FOUR DAYS AFTER her accident, two nurses helped Miss Finch dress and then got her into a wheelchair. Grayson and Alberto wheeled her past the nursing station and down the elevator to the parking garage where Dinah met them. Hugo and Pouncer were waiting in their carrier in the rear seat of the car Dinah drove.

As soon as Miss Finch was situated in the passenger seat, Alberto folded the wheelchair and put it in Dinah's trunk. Grayson pulled Miss Finch's seatbelt over her and clicked it into place.

The hard part came next.

"We'll follow you to Dinah's house and get set up there," Grayson said.

"I won't be going to Dinah's, Grayson."

Grayson frowned. "What do you mean?"

"Please call Alberto over so I might speak to you both at the same time."

Alberto and Grayson squatted beside the open car door, and Miss Finch smiled sadly.

"Gentlemen, I am, with heartfelt thanks, dismissing Gibson Security. Dinah is taking me elsewhere for my convalescent care."

Grayson's forehead furrowed. "You don't mean to tell us where, do you?"

"No, only that it is some distance from here. The fewer who know where I am, the safer I'll be . . . and you, as well."

"I suppose I get it," Alberto said softly, "but . . .

"But we don't like it," Grayson finished.

"Yeah. We don't like it."

"I understand, and I am sorry to leave you in this abrupt manner."

Grayson huffed his frustration. "Well, is there *something* we can do for you? Anything?"

"Yes, thank you for asking. I have two large favors to ask of you, actually." She fumbled in her handbag and retrieved a folded sheet of paper, which she handed to Grayson.

"This is a long and detailed list, but I would like you to hit a large grocery superstore and purchase everything I have listed. Buy enough of those reusable shopping bags to sack the items you buy. I'll pay for the shopping when I pay Gibson Security's last invoice."

Grayson took the paper, perused it, and handed it off to Alberto. "Lady, what are you cooking up? You're not going to need *any* of this stuff for a while."

"Oh, but I need this 'stuff,' as you called it, *now*. As in *immediately*." She fished around in her purse and handed him a second item, a key ring.

"These are the keys to my warehouse, trailer, and car. Please place the shopping bags on my trailer floor."

Grayson took the key ring and stared at it like it might bite him. "Not getting a warm and fuzzy feeling about these tasks."

"'Warm and fuzzy' are not factors vis-à-vis my urgent needs."

"Urgent? But—"

"Tut-tut! Finally, after a number of weeks of healing and when I am ready and signal you, I will need you to deliver my rig to me . . . discreetly."

Alberto and Grayson exchanged glances.

Grayson answered. "You mean keep it off Gibson's books?"

"I think it best to hold these arrangements strictly among the three of us. To put it bluntly, if no one is aware that you have seen me, then that same 'no one' will not attempt to beat my location out of you."

Alberto frowned. "You certainly have a way with words. What about teaching your class?"

"I have collected a number of disposable phones and will videoconference with my class until the quarter ends—although, as another means of distraction, I will instruct my TAs to announce that the videoconferences will be with a substitute rather than with me. My appearance each week will, I hope, be a welcome surprise to my class . . . unless I really do need a substitute on the off occasion.

"My TAs will also administer the final exams and score them, after which I shall access all of my students' scores online and file their grades. Just, as a reminder, if you see an unknown number pop up on your phones in a month or two, it will likely be mine."

Grayson nodded. "Yeah. Okay."

"Thank you again for everything. You have both become . . . very dear to me."

Grayson stared at the parking lot pavement, chewing the inside of his cheek; Alberto acted like he wanted to say something, but he clamped his mouth shut and looked aside instead.

They closed Miss Finch's door.

Dinah drove her away.

FINCH INVESTIGATIONS

CHAPTER 5

THE EARLY EVENING air of late February was much warmer this far south of Los Angeles. Dinah parked the car, a rental, then she and Miss Finch watched as the medical facility closed up for the day and the last patients and the staff departed.

When the clinic, with the exception of a dim light within the lobby, was dark, Dinah's phone received a text. "Here we go."

Leaving Hugo and Pouncer in the car with the windows cracked, Dinah got out, retrieved the wheelchair from her trunk, helped Miss Finch into it, and rolled it up to the clinic's main entrance. A woman opened the door and waved them inside. She locked the door behind her.

"Nice to see you again, Dinah."

"You, as well, Myra." Dinah turned to Miss Finch. "This is Myra, Dr. Sepúlveda's office manager. Myra, this is the friend I spoke of."

"A pleasure to meet you," Myra replied. "Please follow me to my office."

No mention of my name, Miss Finch realized.

Myra led the way down a shadowed hallway to her office. After Dinah had wheeled Miss Finch inside, Myra closed the door and switched on the light.

"I apologize for the 'cloak and dagger,' but we take security seriously. Do make yourselves comfortable." She then spoke to Miss Finch. "Although your situation differs significantly from our other patients requiring anonymity, we sympathize with your plight. Dr. Sepúlveda has agreed to take you on."

Miss Finch nodded. "Thank you. Dinah gave me to understand that you provide medical care for survivors of domestic violence."

"That's correct. Dinah has been a vital part of our little underground movement for quite some time."

"So she told me. She also said you have a method of concealing these victims' identities?"

"Yes, simple but effective. When we finish talking, I will assign you a preexisting identity in our computer system, after which you will have your initial appointment with Dr. Sepúlveda, who is presently waiting for you in his office.

"Whenever you return to us for treatment or physical therapy, you will check in using your assigned identity. Your record in our system has a flag attached to it that allows you to check in without showing the clerk any identifying documentation."

"I see. And how is payment handled?"

"We do not charge the survivors who come to us. From you, however, we will accept an electronic funds transfer, payment in full, from the account of your choice—but not until six months after your treatment is complete. Do you agree to our terms?"

"A wise strategy. Yes, I agree."

Myra folded her hands together. "Full disclosure here: We cannot guarantee that our computer system or processes are foolproof. For the most part, the women we serve are pursued by men lacking the means or technical sophistication to track them. If I understand correctly, your situation puts our clinic at higher risk. Is this correct?"

Miss Finch nodded. "Those looking for me have deep pockets, and deep pockets can buy, as you put it, sophisticated technical resources. Will you know if your system is hacked?"

"I believe so. That said, relationships with our special patients are usually of a short-term nature. We treat their wounds once or twice, perhaps three times, before our organization resettles them in other states with new identities. We immediately save their patient history to a backup drive, but wipe their identity from our system. Given the short window of vulnerability, the risk is low."

Myra looked at Miss Finch. "Your rehabilitation, on the other hand, will take weeks, perhaps months. That keeps you in our system far longer than usual and increases your risk. I should also tell you—and Dr.

Sepúlveda will repeat this caveat—while he is a surgeon, he is not an ankle specialist. We can see you through your convalescence and PT, but should complications arise requiring a specialist, we would not be able to help you."

"I understand."

"Very good. Let's introduce you to Dr. Sepúlveda, shall we?"

———————●———————

WHEN MISS FINCH finished her appointment with the doctor, Myra handed them a slip of paper with a phone number on it. "Dinah, I am assuming you followed procedure, that you and our guest ditched your phones so they cannot be used to trace you here?"

Dinah nodded. "My usual phone is at home."

"I left my phone behind also," Miss Finch responded.

"Good. Tell the woman who answers at this number that I sent you. She maintains several vacation rentals, one in particular that is kept available for our network's use. For safety's sake, she accepts cash only. Will that be a problem?"

Miss Finch reflected briefly on the "go" bag she had assembled months ago and stashed with Dinah. The bag was presently in the rental car's trunk, and she had added to it before leaving the hospital. It contained everything she would need in a short-term "pinch"—a large amount of cash, her collection of burner phones, a change of clothes, personal hygiene items, first aid kit, pain meds, the sidearm she legally possessed as a California-licensed PI, two boxes of ammo, two bottles of water, and emergency rations for Hugo, Pouncer, and herself. Aside from the bag, she also had the laptop Grayson and Alberto had salvaged from the wreckage of her Range Rover and copies of her medical records from the hospital.

From here on out, that bag must accompany me wherever I go: house, car, appointments, and so on. In point of fact, I should have brought it into the clinic with me.

"Cash will not be a problem," Miss Finch murmured.

"Then I look forward to seeing you when you return for your next appointment."

———————●———————

OUT IN THE PARKING lot, Dinah helped Miss Finch into the car and placed the folded wheelchair in her trunk. When she had seated herself in the car, she keyed in the number Myra had given them and put her phone on speaker. They spoke to the woman on the other end, and Miss Finch scribbled down verbal directions to the rental.

"I am impressed," Miss Finch murmured when they hit the road. "This network has a thorough, well-conceived methodology."

"They have learned through the years what works and, sadly, what does not. Not all of their survivors successfully evaded their abusers."

"Despicable!"

"Yes, but what did Dr. Sepúlveda say when he examined you?"

"He congratulated me on my vast and colorful array of bruises."

Dinah giggled. "Did he truly?"

"*No*. The man had the audacity to tell me he'd seen worse."

Dinah's giggles turned to laughter. "Honestly, BD, sometimes your sarcasm verges on the criminal."

"Only *verges?* I must really up my game."

"Stop! I can't fall over laughing and still drive. Besides, I want to know what the doctor actually said."

"He said the cut on my arm is healing nicely. Stitches should come out next week."

"And when he saw your ankle?"

"Not much to see with my foot and calf in a cast, but I did present him with the copies of my X-rays and MRI. He spent several minutes going over them, then estimated my cast should come off in another five weeks. Apparently, I will start my physical therapy the same day."

"How long will you do PT?"

"Depends on how I do. Several weeks at a minimum."

"And how long will you need me to stay with you?"

Miss Finch grimaced. "You have done so much already; I hate to inconvenience you further, Dinah."

"Nonsense. This is what friends are for. How long did the doctor say you would need a caretaker?"

Miss Finch's mouth turned down. "Until I can do for myself without assistance. He did assure me I will be feeling much more like myself in a a week or two. I suppose we can reevaluate then." She sighed. "My class will keep me occupied for a few more weeks, and I have a couple of phone appointments I cannot miss. I can also work on my second book. All that aside, I am not looking forward to being cooped up for weeks on end."

"How about a number of short road trips to see the local sights? What do you think of that idea?"

"I think you are a gem, Dinah."

CHAPTER 6

THE SUCCEEDING TWO weeks progressed slowly for Miss Finch, particularly dealing with her body's pains and discomfort as her various bruises, scrapes, and strains from the "accident" healed. Dinah bought packages of frozen peas to use as cold compresses. They helped, but not with her ankle's swelling and pain within the cast.

To distract herself, Miss Finch taught her class via videoconference viewed in the auditorium on a large-screen and worked on her second book's draft. Dinah also took the two of them on several short road trips, while Miss Finch learned to get around on crutches—*children's* crutches. By the end of those first two weeks, she was feeling much better and was fairly confident she could manage without Dinah's assistance.

The most pressing need following Dinah's departure would be how best to acquire a temporary car for Miss Finch and still maintain her anonymity. Myra again presented them with a solution.

"We have a member within our San Diego network who can loan you a car. It won't be fancy, of course, and a modest fee is necessary to cover the car's upkeep. Give me a date, and someone will deliver the vehicle to your rental hostess, who will receive the fee from you in exchange for the car's keys. You will never see the car's delivery driver, and the driver will never see you."

"The more I learn about your network, the more impressed I am," Miss Finch murmured.

"Thank you. In addition to your payment for our services, would you consider making a donation so that we might continue providing payment-free support to domestic abuse victims?"

"Yes. You may count on it."

The car was delivered two days later.

After Miss Finch demonstrated she could manage herself, her crutches, and the car to Dinah's satisfaction, they said goodbye.

"You will let me know how you're getting on?" Dinah asked.

"I'll call your burner phone from one of my burner phones. If you do not answer, I'll send a pithy text concerning your car's extended warranty as a signal that all is well."

They had a good laugh and hugged.

"You are quite weary from caring for me, my friend," Miss Finch whispered. "Thank you for all you have done for me and my darlings. When you get home, I hope you will treat yourself to a good rest."

"Trust me, I will. Aruba, here I come!"

———•———

NEARLY THREE WEEKS after the attempt on her life, Miss Finch taught her final class of the quarter. She was astounded when, at the end of the period, the students overflowing the auditorium—and her three TAs—stood *en masse* to applaud and cheer her.

Dr. Normandy was also present, clapping with tepid enthusiasm. He could not help but shake his head at the students' open affection for Miss Finch. He flinched when he heard the low chant begin.

POUN-cer!

POUN-cer!

POUN-cer!

POUN-cer!

Foot stomping joined the demand.

POUNCER! POUNCER! POUNCER!

Miss Finch laughed aloud, then murmured, "Here, Pouncer."

Pouncer leaped upon her shoulder, wrapped herself around the back of Miss Finch's neck until she lay crosswise, lifted her nose, and preened—to the cheers of the filled auditorium.

But the students were not finished.

HUGO! HUGO! HUGO!

"Here, Hugo."

Hugo pressed his nose against the screen of Miss Finch's phone. On the other end, his wet nose, then his eyes filled the auditorium's entire screen—to the students' great, laughing delight and applause.

When Miss Finch was finally able to curb her students' wholehearted approval, she said, "I thank you. Pouncer and Hugo thank you. And with that, I wish you a fond *adieu*," and clicked off the call.

After the auditorium emptied, the class TAs retired to the office the university had assigned Miss Finch and to their personal videoconference with her. She instructed them on the administration of the class's final exam the following week.

"You have done well," she told them to their blushing faces. "You have grown through the quarter and our rather unorthodox process, and I am proud of each of you. I could not have done this without you."

———————●———————

WHILE CLOSING OUT the quarter, Miss Finch had used up her stash of disposable phones. Later that day, she headed east on I-8 toward El Centro. The town had multiple truck stops within the radius of a few blocks. She intended to buy a dozen phones, split among three or four of the truck stops.

"Good thing they call these 'disposable' phones," she spoke over her shoulder to Hugo, "since I only use one a few times before ditching it."

She checked the road ahead and behind them. So far, so good.

"I cannot be too careful when it comes to Don Massimo and the Lucchese Family, since Tony Massimo died trying to kill us—you and Pouncer included. The Don could very well blame me for his son's death."

After making her purchases, she followed 86 north then 78 west. Along a particularly barren stretch of road, she pulled over. She had removed and snapped in pieces the SIM cards from her old phones. Now she scattered the bits in the desert just off the shoulder. The phones themselves she had gathered into a paper sack. She drove on, indulged in a pleasant lunch in Ramona, and on the outskirts of San Diego, dropped the sack into a public recycle bin for electronics.

Feeling "clean" again, she returned to the house she occupied.

———————●———————

THE FOLLOWING DAY, she again drove far out on I-8. She pulled over outside Ocotillo to call the FBI agent tasked with ensuring that Miss Finch's testimony against the Lucchese Family remained alive and intact.

Grayson hadn't been wrong when he remarked that Miss Finch held her secrets close to the vest: Not one of Miss Finch's acquaintances or friends, not even Dinah, knew Miss Finch had provided the FBI with copies of the evidence she'd collected against Don Massimo and his organization. Neither was it known that *she* would be the DOJ's star witness when it convened a grand jury to indict Massimo and take him to trial.

If the DOJ ever makes it that far, she thought.

The DOJ's prosecution processes, as she was finding out the hard way, were laborious, cumbersome, and entirely unpredictable. While she waited for her summons to testify, Miss Finch focused on survival—at least up to and through giving her testimony before the grand jury.

I should be safe enough to go about my life afterward. But even if I am wrong? Even if Don Massimo puts a hit on me after the fact? I no longer care. I have already determined that bringing him and his organization to justice is well worth the price of my life.

At this point in her internal ruminations, Miss Finch shut down. She didn't care to revisit her motives for going after Don Massimo and his organization. *That* pain, unlike her physical ailments, while softening over time, was never going to leave.

"It does not mean I wish my life cut short," she whispered. "I am taking and will continue to take every precaution until I have given testimony before the grand jury."

Her FBI handler had wanted to put her in witness protection, had insisted the US Marshals Service would keep her safe. Miss Finch declined their services.

Actually, I ditched the Marshals' help, she admitted, *and will keep my whereabouts as much a secret from them and the FBI as from everyone else in my life.* Not only was such "help" incredibly restrictive, but she had seen too many movies where law enforcement leaked like the proverbial sieve.

I am not about to trust my well-being and longevity to the Justice Department's ponderous, ill-reputed bureaucracy.

What Miss Finch needed from her handler, the reason for her call, was news on when the DOJ would empanel the grand jury to indict Don Massimo and his lieutenants. That date had been at the top of Miss Finch's need-to-know list for months—right up until Antony Massimo tried to run her over with a tanker truck. Since then, staying alive had taken precedence.

Still, the only way out of her messy predicament was to successfully get through the trial—which took her back to needing the date the DOJ would empanel the grand jury. It was why she now broke with her own security protocols to call her FBI handler, Special Agent Andrea Claussen.

"Andrea'*!'*"

"Miss Finch! Where in the world are—"

"Never mind where I am. Make note of this number. It is a 'burner' as I believe you people call prepaid phones. Since I do not wish to be hunted or hounded, I will turn this phone on *only* to check for messages from you—and this is the only method of communication I will allow between us. Is that clear?"

"Yes, I have the number, but—"

"Andrea, has the prosecutor set a date to convene the grand jury?"

"We're working on it with him."

She felt her anger rise. "You are *working* on it? You mean to say the date is still undetermined? Of all the *foolish, bureaucratic*—"

"Miss Finch, hold up a minute! Where are you? I need to be able to tell my superiors that you're okay."

"Please pardon this old woman's feeble mind, *Agent Claussen,* but I find *zero* correlation between your need to know my whereabouts and my continued well-being!"

"But you were seriously injured and disappeared on us!"

"Of course, I was seriously injured. *You* try getting bulldozed by a tanker truck! And *of course*, I disappeared. But, again, how would your superiors' knowledge of my whereabouts improve my personal safety? Frankly, I am convinced I would be *less* safe should they know where I am."

"Why, that's ridiculous and absurd!"

"Ah! Shall I tell you why it is neither ridiculous nor absurd? Don Massimo would never have sanctioned Antony's quite public move against me. The Don is far too clever to commit murder in the open, nor would he risk his son's life in such a brazen and dangerous attack. The Don's *son*, however, is—or rather *was*—neither as cautious nor as smart as his father. No, the last stupid act of Antony Massimo's life was his personally motivated and ill-conceived attempt to kill me because of how I painted him in my book."

She lowered her voice. "That said, as imprudent and reckless as Tony Massimo proved himself to be, he was still his father's only son, his heir. So, just who do you think Don Massimo blames? And would the Don, in this or any other universe, ever allow his son's death to go unavenged?"

"Miss Finch, please listen—"

"No, *you* listen! Before Tony Massimo's death, the Don was after me to pull my book from the market. He used his goons to threaten me and threaten my publisher. He put a tracker on my car and left ominous 'gifts' next to my mailbox. Now ask yourself these questions: Is it possible that Don Massimo suspects the DOJ is building a case against him? That I have provided the FBI with reams of evidence on the operations of the LA branch of the Lucchese Family? Or that I am your 'star' witness when the DOJ convenes a grand jury? Given those suppositions and the fact his son died trying to kill me, does the Don now have less *or more* reason to seek me out?"

"But these are baseless and outlandish imaginings, Miss Finch!"

Whispering, Miss Finch replied, "Perhaps they are; oh, I pray they are. However, should any of my 'baseless and outlandish imaginings' be true, just where do you think the Don would go first to obtain information on my whereabouts?"

Claussen's tone chilled. "What are you insinuating?"

"I apologize for my ambiguity, my lack of clarity. Let me try to be less obtuse and more pellucid: I have managed to disappear—*poof!*—right into thin air, so who will the Don immediately suspect of whisking me away? Only two bureaucracies have such 'power' at their fingertips: the FBI and the US Marshals Service. The only question remaining, then, is which organization has Don Massimo penetrated?"

"What a convoluted and preposterous accusation!"

"Convoluted? Perhaps. Preposterous? Not in the slightest. So, if you don't mind, *Agent Claussen*, I will keep my whereabouts to myself. Have I finally made myself clear?"

Miss Finch heard Claussen's furious breathing through the phone and waited for the woman to respond. When Claussen finally did answer, it was to stiffly mutter, "If someone in my division is dirty, as you, without a shred of proof, are suggesting, I will get to the bottom of it."

Miss Finch put her car in gear and left Ocotillo. Instead of reentering I-8, she crossed it and drove south on Imperial Highway, while trying to stuff her anger back into its proper place. She soon reached the turnoff to CA-98, turned left, and headed southeast.

"Miss Finch? Did you hear me? I will *quietly* investigate and uncover the facts of the matter. You have my word."

"I expect no less from you, Andrea. Now tell me the truth: Are you, as we speak, using this call to track my location?"

Claussen sighed. "We had your general location east of San Diego and see that you are now on the move. But please don't worry; I promise to keep this information tightly controlled."

Miss Finch laughed with bitter humor. "Unless, of course, you are already compromised. You say you will investigate? Then *follow the money*, Andrea. Without a doubt, a traitor in your midst would be receiving payment to determine and pass on my location. Find the money, find the conspirators."

Miss Finch punched the "End Call" button and powered off the phone. She continued thinking on the situation as she flipped a U-turn and headed back toward San Diego, sorting through the details of her situation she could influence . . . and the much larger parts beyond her control. "I must not use this burner to call Agent Claussen again. However, I need to keep it with me so I can check for any messages she might leave. No one can track a quick on and a quick off."

FINCH INVESTIGATIONS

CHAPTER 7

MARCH PASSED UNEVENTFULLY, and April arrived. With it, south Cali's weather warmed nicely. Miss Finch, on crutches, gimped along outside twice each day, going as far as her stamina would allow her.

"This is the only exercise I can get, but it is better than sitting around, stagnating and losing muscle mass," she grumbled on her second outing of the day. "It does not change the fact that, with my class over, I am bored out of my ever-loving mind."

At least she could look forward to having her cast removed on Thursday of the following week. That same day, she would begin her physical therapy—the therapy Dr. Sepúlveda had warned would likely prove somewhat painful.

"I am not an orthopedic surgeon; foot and ankle injuries are not my specialty, Gladys," he said, using her assigned clinic persona. "In my quite limited experience, an ankle's healing process is complicated by the fact that the foot and ankle have many bones. Translation? Lots of moving parts and pieces. The truth is, repairing all the broken pieces resulting from an accident such as yours is one thing; getting all the repaired pieces to 'play nice' with each other is another."

"I . . . suppose I understand."

"*Bueno*. That said, I should also remind you that should you experience post-surgical problems, I would not be able to treat you for those issues. You would need to find a good foot surgeon for further care."

"Yes, I am clear on that point."

Yeah, yeah, she groused inwardly. *I'll be fine. Just get me out of this cast! I cannot wait to actually* walk *again.*

In the meantime, she fired up the burner designated for Special Agent Claussen once daily, hoping for a message from the woman. As of yet, though, she had heard nothing from her.

If Andrea actually has a leak in her division and cannot eliminate it, how much longer will I be safe here?

———— ◦ ————

THE DAY MISS FINCH looked forward to finally arrived. She practically hummed with excitement as Dr. Sepúlveda's assistant cut the cast from her foot and calf. However, the sight of her newly freed appendage was daunting.

"Oh, dear."

I am grieved to report that you closely resemble a death camp survivor, she informed her emaciated limb, *or perhaps some albino creature recently crawled up from the dark recesses of the earth?*

"Not to worry, Gladys," the doctor's assistant said, reading her expression. "Everyone has the same reaction. By this time next week, the dead, dry skin will have sloughed off, and your leg and foot will have regained a little color and muscle tone."

"From your mouth to God's ear," she murmured, studying the ugly scar left by the surgery to repair her ankle.

Dr. Sepúlveda entered the exam room and gently manipulated her foot. "Any pain or discomfort, Gladys?"

"Not as yet."

"I'm going to rotate your ankle a bit more aggressively. Let me know if it hurts. Anything?"

"No, but everything feels . . . quite stiff."

"To be expected. I'll turn you over to the PT department now. You'll be wearing an orthopedic boot for a while, and I'll see you again in about four weeks."

A boot? And four weeks? *Four weeks!* Her bubble of giddy anticipation uttered a pathetic *pop* and plummeted to earth.

Yet another clinic employee took Dr. Sepúlveda's place.

"Hi, Gladys. I'm Sean, your physical therapist. Let's get your boot fitted, then we'll do a bit of gentle walking."

Fifteen minutes later, he wheeled her and her booted foot up to a walkway between two rails. "I'll help you stand. You grab hold of the bars, put your weight on both feet, then walk to the other side. Don't rush; just take your time."

Miss Finch stood. She reached for the bars, steadied herself, and began to walk. She sighed as her left foot, weak from the cast's confinement, protested a little. Slowly, grateful for the boot's support, she made her way to the end of the rails and back.

"How was that?" Sean asked.

"Not too bad, actually."

"Great! Let's get on with today's therapy. When we're done, we'll get you scheduled for PT three days a week. I'll send you home with exercises to do there too. Don't push yourself too hard at first. Oh, and Gladys? No more crutches. From this time forward, we want you to use a walker. Later, you'll move to a cane until you are fully stable on your feet."

"I have graduated from crutches to a walker? And can look forward to a cane? My, where do I pick up such flattering accoutrements?"

Sean grinned. "Oh, we have the latest styles and colors right here. Trust me: You'll be all the rage."

She made a face. "I am certain I will."

Sean laughed. He brought her a walker and sized it to fit her. Then he ran her through several simple exercises and sent them to an app on her phone so she could follow them at home. When they finished, she accompanied him to the scheduling computer, gaining confidence with each step—until she came to an abrupt halt and leaned on the right side of the walker to take her weight off her booted left foot.

"Ow, ow, ow!"

"What's wrong?"

"Something sharp stabbed me!"

"I'm sorry, but such pain as you describe is not uncommon. Just remember that, in addition to having broken many bones, you also suffered significant soft tissue damage."

"That did not feel like soft tissue damage."

He nodded patiently. "Gladys, you have oodles of damaged nerves and nerve endings within your soft tissues. Those nerves take time to regenerate and may cause sharp, stinging pains as they do so. In the meantime, please be patient with your body and continue the exercises I've given you, plus regular, easy walking. Don't worry; I'm confident that with physical therapy and the passage of time, you will get through this."

Miss Finch gingerly put her weight back on her booted foot. "If you say so."

KEEPING UP WITH her daily physical therapy exercises plus the required twice-daily "gentle walking" was grueling, often painful work. After two weeks of PT, she was weary of it all—the drudgery, the lack of mobility, and the sharp pain in her ankle that, like a phantom in the night, ambushed her again and again.

"You so-called 'regenerating' nerve endings are about to get my goat!" she shouted in her living room, "but hear this! I am no quitter, and I promise: I *will* outlast you."

She pressed on with determination, distracted and concerned that she had heard nothing from Agent Claussen. The silence and uncertainty were making her jumpy.

I need to plan my next move. Be ready to go at a moment's notice.

"Lord," she prayed, "While I fully recover, I think it would be wise for me to hole up over the summer in some location where I can blend in as just another unremarkable vacationer. Would you please lead me to the right place?"

She browsed the internet for destinations meeting her criteria, running multiple scenarios and plotting logistics in her head. "What would work best is a resort town where summer tourism is an absolute madhouse and one more camper will hardly be remarkable."

Using Google Maps, she explored possibilities due east of San Diego. She rejected Arizona, New Mexico, and Texas out of hand.

"Too hot in the summer. Besides, I believe I would prefer a mountain refuge under tall pine trees, somewhere teeming with vacationers."

She moved north of California into Oregon and Washington, but wasn't familiar enough with the suggested areas to judge them against her criteria.

"Perhaps a mountain lake?"

She moved her cursor farther east. Idaho had Lake Coeur d'Alene and Lake Pend Oreille, while Montana had Flathead Lake—but neither of those lakes was quite as overrun with crowds of tourists as she hoped to find and blend into. She was navigating back into California when a body of water caught her eye.

Lake Tahoe. Sometimes called "Big Blue."

"Hello! Why, Tahoe is a perfect rat race of tourism during the summer," she murmured, "and a perfect rat race makes Tahoe an absolutely *perfect* hideaway . . . that is, if I can locate and reserve the right sort of RV space."

She explored her search results and discarded state and federal campgrounds that had a 14-day stay limit.

"I can't be hopping from campground to campground twice a month. Why, even finding a campsite during the summer is impossible. No. I need something more long-term."

She was studying Tahoe RV parks with monthly leases, shaking her head at their tiny cheek-by-jowl sites with zero privacy, when a flashy ad popped up:

BRIGHT STAR
SUMMER RV RESIDENCE
Located Near South Lake Tahoe

"Hmm. What's the difference between a summer residence and an RV park? What can that distinction mean?" She clicked on the link, found herself on Bright Star's landing page, and read the site's description.

Welcome to *the* unique Lake Tahoe experience,
Bright Star Summer RV Residence!

Tired of the crush, traffic, and noise
of common, everyday RV parks?
At **Bright Star**, you will enjoy the privacy and beauty
of your own secluded mountain site
for the entire summer season.

At **Bright Star**, we offer 24 *exclusive* RV sites,
all sites nestled under a canopy of tall pine trees.
Each site is 40 feet from its nearest neighboring site,
ensuring all residents enjoy an entire summer of
privacy and tranquil solitude.

At **Bright Star,** we provide full RV hookups, cable,
internet, and ample in-site parking for your RV,
your other vehicles, and a complimentary golf cart.

At **Bright Star**, each site has its own paved patio area
with firepit, barbecue, picnic table,
and chilled drinking water dispenser,
surrounded by a maintained lawn.

Every **Bright Star** resident **and their guests** may
enjoy our brand-new, state-of-the-art swimming complex,
complete with family pool and water slides,
separate toddler splash pool, and an adult-only lap pool.
Enjoy a fully stocked rec center, a group barbecue area,
pickleball and volleyball courts, and much, much more.

"Stay for the whole summer? I like that idea!"

Miss Finch devoured the details and feasted on the photographs. She dug deeper, looking for the cost. She gaped when she found the staggering amount.

Holy spumoni! Pay up-front for the entire season, hey? The owners were certainly not kidding about the "exclusive" part either. Summer at Bright Star calls for a mighty hefty chunk of change.

She sat back and thought it through. "Yes, it's exorbitant, but the price would be worth it should it guarantee me a *private* RV site from Memorial Day weekend through Labor Day. No nosy neighbors watching my every move or blaring their music in my face. I would enjoy the peace and quiet, and Hugo and Pouncer would love the space."

She clicked on Bright Star's map and studied the road winding gracefully through the park. Inside the road was an "island" marked with the park's swimming complex and other touted amenities. Along the road's outside perimeter were the widely spaced twenty-four RV sites, each site labeled either "available" or "taken."

She gaped again when she realized the majority of the sites were already taken—that only five of the twenty-four sites remained available.

"Merciful heavens. I need to act quickly!"

She clicked on the application process detailing Bright Star's requirements and nearly choked.

"Oh, dear—this will never work!"

She went over the list several times, reading each requirement aloud.

"Resident RVs must be a minimum of thirty feet in length.

"Resident RVs must be no older than seven years.

"Resident RVs must be clean and well-maintained with no noticeable neglect, damage, missing parts, or discoloration to the frame or paint.

"Resident RVs must be leveled and skirted within 24 hours of arrival.

"Resident RV systems must be compatible with and connected to Bright Star's electrical, water, and septic systems within 24 hours of arrival and during the entirety of the residency period.

"Residents must maintain their RV and assigned site in a manner that reflects and honors the spirit of Bright Star Summer RV Residence."

Well, Lord? While my pretty little travel trailer meets most of the requirements, it fails the first two in spectacular fashion . . . unless a complete renovation allows my trailer to be considered "new." Nevertheless, my rig could never be mistaken for thirty feet in length. You would need to perform yet another miracle for my RV to qualify at this "exclusive" park.

Unwilling to let go of what had seemed like the perfect answer to her prayers, she clicked on the lease agreement and began to read it aloud.

"By completing this lease agreement in full and by pressing the 'Submit' button, I, *insert name here*, enter into a binding agreement with Bright Star Summer RV Residence, LLC and its owners, Joseph and Holly Mitchell—"

She stared at the page. "Joseph Mitchell? As in Joe Mitchell?"

Goosebumps prickled up her arms and down the back of her neck.

"Heavenly days! Could it be? No, not likely. After all, neither Joseph nor Mitchell are uncommon names, and the world must contain hundreds of Joe Mitchells, yes? I mean, what are the odds *this* Joe Mitchell would be the one Joe Mitchell I knew, all those years ago?"

But the weird thing was, Miss Finch was nearly certain "her" Joe Mitchell had mentioned his fiancée back in the States, a girl named Holly.

Her mind tugged on a memory more than thirty-five years in the past. In response, the faint layout of a US military hospital in Germany rose to the surface. She had volunteered for six months at that hospital during the First Gulf War. While serving at the hospital, she had comforted and consoled many a wounded soldier. She ran errands, read books and magazines aloud, wrote letters . . . and came to know a young man by the name of Joe Mitchell.

"It was such a long time ago, Lord, and he was dreadfully injured at the time. Will he remember me? Would he recall the favor I did for his buddy, his best friend . . . a soldier who didn't make it home from the battlefield?"

Miss Finch studied the online map of the RV park once more. She started at Bright Star's office, with its imposing front gate, and traced the route through the RV park and the twenty-four sites sprouting from the road's outside periphery. She examined the photo montage for each available site, the images providing a glimpse into the site's size, shape, and amenities. Her eyes locked onto the park's first site, set far back from the road, and the attached photo of a little sun-dappled stream as it meandered through the trees beyond the back of the site.

"I would like this one, Lord . . . if it is your will for me. It would be pleasant to open my windows and hear the burbling sound of the creek as its water cascades over rocks on its merry way."

She sighed and clicked out of the map. Returned to the page listing Bright Star's contact information. She set her mouth resolutely and punched the number into her current general-use phone.

"Lord Jesus, I trust you. I will ask, seek, and knock; if you want me to have this site, you will make a way where there doesn't seem to be a way."

She hit the call button. A woman answered.

"Bright Star Summer RV Residence, Holly speaking. May I help you?"

"Good morning. May I speak with Mr. Joe Mitchell, please?"

"I'm Holly Mitchell, Joe's wife and Bright Star's office manager. Perhaps I could assist you?"

"Thank you for your kind offer, but I would prefer to speak to Mr. Mitchell."

"Unfortunately, he is out of the office. May I take a message?"

"Yes, please. Would you give him my number and ask him to return my call?"

"Of course. And who is calling?"

"Tell him . . . an old acquaintance is calling. Thank you."

———— ❖ ————

MISS FINCH HUNG UP. Would the man actually call back? And if he did call, would he be the Joe Mitchell, out of all the Joe Mitchells in the world, who owed her . . . a little favor?

She waited the remainder of the day on pins and needles until, early that evening, her phone rang.

"Hello?"

"Yes, hello. This is Joe Mitchell from Bright Star Summer RV Residence returning your call."

The voice was familiar, and chills raced down BD's spine.

"Joe . . . this is BD Finch."

A startled gasp rang from the phone.

"Miss Finch? Is it you? Truly?"

"Truly, old friend. How are you?"

"Right as rain—and so happy to hear from you! Miss Finch, I will never be able to thank you enough for what you . . . you know."

"Did everything work out? Have you kept in contact?"

"Yes, it did work out, thank God. Rob's family took her . . . and Rob's baby into their home and family. They have never regretted it."

"Ah! Well, then, I am pleased to have helped."

"But I owe you, Miss Finch. I solemnly promised I would return the favor someday. So, what can I do for you?"

"Now that you have mentioned it, Joe, there is something."

"Anything. You name it."

"Very well. I would like a berth at your lovely park this summer—I will pay in full for it, of course, no problem there. However, I would need your assistance overcoming two little hurdles having to do with the RV requirements."

She explained in detail. He listened and asked questions.

In the end, he said, "I will do it, Miss Finch. However, I should be candid with you. Holly, my wife, is quite insistent that we uphold the requirements. She would reject your submission straight off, should you apply online. Instead, I will make certain exceptions to the rules and application, initial and sign them, and email a PDF copy to you. When you receive the revised lease, sign it, finish filling out the application, and email both back to me."

He cleared his throat. "Holly and I have separate email addresses. When I receive the completed application and signed lease, I will log into our site as an administrator, reserve the site of your choice, and trigger the payment request. Once you've paid for your site, you will receive a confirmation email. I will let Holly know about the exceptions I have made."

"Thank you, Joe."

"Would you care for anything else, Miss Finch? Truly, anything at all?"

"Well . . ." Miss Finch drew out the word while plotting how she might overcome the last few obstacles standing between her, a clean getaway from San Diego, and her safe, unnoticed arrival at South Lake Tahoe.

Joe said softly, "I do mean anything, Miss Finch."

"Joe, you are a dear man and kindness itself. If I understand correctly, check-in begins the Thursday prior to Memorial Day weekend. Would it be possible for me to check in on Wednesday, a day early?"

"I will make it happen. Now, may I have your email address? And which site would you prefer? I will reserve it for you."

"Site 1, if you please, Joe. And thank you again."

"Miss Finch, it is the least I can do for the great favor you did for me and for . . . Rob. I look forward to seeing you again."

"And I you, Joe."

———◆———

TWO EVENINGS LATER, she opened an email from Joe. She filled out the attached application on the spot, signed it, then reviewed and signed the amended lease agreement. She emailed the two files back to Joe.

Done.

Her next steps needed additional forethought: When to leave San Diego, where to meet Grayson and Alberto to collect her car and trailer, and how to return the loaner car to Myra's organization.

Those steps became more urgent when she powered on the phone she had dedicated to Special Agent Claussen and found a voicemail.

"Miss Finch, you were right. Someone in Don Massimo's organization has an informant inside our division, but since we weren't successful in tracing you, neither we nor they have your location. Power off your phone as soon as you listen to this message, then sit tight wherever you are and remain vigilant. I will leave another update in a day or two."

FINCH
INVESTIGATIONS

CHAPTER 8

AS APRIL MOVED into May, the weather grew balmy and more pleasant. Miss Finch also graduated from a walker to a cane, and she took to driving to the beach each afternoon. She packed a towel and additional food and drink into her go bag and transferred the bag to the car. Next, she loaded Hugo and Pouncer into their rear seats, hoisted their rolling carrier into the trunk, and laid a folded beach umbrella across the floor.

At their favorite beach, she put Hugo and Pouncer into their carrier, slung the beach umbrella and her go bag over her shoulder, grabbed the carrier's handle in one hand and her cane in the other, then hobbled her way down a boardwalk to the beach.

After settling their things under the umbrella and releasing Hugo and Pouncer, Miss Finch and her pets ambled along the shoreline, where the damp sand gave her feet firmer purchase than the dry sand. She "ambled" because the sharp pain in her ankle, occasionally absent, other times incessant, kept her wary and on guard.

She also "ambled" because Scan warned her after every PT appointment, "Don't risk a fall while you are healing, Gladys. Be cautious and careful."

Careful, careful, careful.

I am sick of careful!

And my name is not Gladys; it is BD Finch, she groused to herself, weary of her constraints.

Nevertheless, she *was* cautious, dutiful to do her required exercises and twice-daily walking while trying not to awaken the inexplicable on-again, off-again pain in her ankle. After her slow walk up and down the shore, she spent the remainder of their stay seated on a piece of driftwood, reading, or on a towel under the umbrella, watching while Hugo and Pouncer raced up and down the shoreline.

She never worried about them; they were quite inseparable and did not stray far from her, Pouncer behaving more like a dog than a cat in most regards. Either Pouncer rode atop Hugo, surveying her domain through bored, slitted eyes, or together, Hugo and Pouncer chased after the ebb and flow of the frothy waves on the sand and inevitably dragged or carried to her whatever they found as the waves receded.

Hugo loved to proudly drop and display his finds in front of Miss Finch, tongue hanging out to the side of his happy smile. Pouncer, as was her custom, took the more direct approach, apparently believing Miss Finch would appreciate her discoveries "up close and personal," said treasures generally composed of things once alive but now quite "de" composed.

Miss Finch shuddered. Hugo brought Miss Finch pretty rocks, sticks of all sizes and shapes, and the occasional tin can or other shiny trash, whereas Pouncer's latest offering had been a decaying seagull—which she proudly plopped into Miss Finch's lap.

She shuddered again. "Ugh!"

While she rested at the beach, Miss Finch also checked her "Agent Claussen" burner for updates, but none came. The longer the silence stretched, the more concerned and vigilant she grew. Her vigilance compelled her to keep track of other beachgoers, particularly anyone alone or who appeared more than once. She watched them over the pages of her book, while standing to stretch and call Hugo and Pouncer in from their frolics for a drink of water, or by turning her small pair of binoculars from the sea to those individuals who warranted closer examination.

And before returning home each day, she checked Agent Claussen's phone for messages—still finding nothing—then drove cautiously up her street, past her driveway, and around the block. As she passed her present abode, she inspected it and scrutinized any person or vehicle on the street unfamiliar to her, all while applying her physical therapist's warnings of "be cautious and careful" more to her personal security than to her ankle's well-being.

"*Pfft!* You've become afraid of your own shadow, BD Finch," she chided herself. "How on earth could Don Massimo's people ever track you here, anyway?"

But her cynical side responded, "And yet, the *how* won't matter a whit if they find you out—will it?"

"True," she sighed.

Don Massimo had wealth and power. He could announce a bounty on her head, and one hundred "head" hunters would hit the streets within the hour. Eventually, some money-hungry apex predator might sniff out the slightest lead within her circle of friends and acquaintances. Apply enough pressure, and something was bound to crack.

Meaning that a bounty hunter could be on her faster than Pouncer on a scuttling sand crab.

Her growing unease over Agent Claussen's silence was why, near the end of the first full week of May, she finally powered on an unused burner, called Grayson, added Alberto to the call, and rehearsed her next steps with them.

The two of them, however, refused to listen until they had thoroughly vented over her silence.

"Miss Finch, we've been worried sick about you. Are you all right?" Grayson asked in a near-shout. "Why, you haven't called even *once!*"

"You have no idea how worried we've been!" Alberto added. "Haven't heard a word from you in over two months!"

She was surprised. Confounded even.

"You have been worried? About me?"

Grayson snorted. "Ya think? Even your friend Dinah declares she hasn't heard from you."

"Of course she has not! And while I am quite sorry to have kept the three of you in the dark, I did it *for* you, not to spite you."

Her voice softened. "I simply could not risk calling before now, my sole intent is to protect *you* from harm due to your association with me. I really could not live with myself should Don Massimo torture you to extract information I made certain you did not possess. You do understand my reasoning, do you not?"

"I suppose," Grayson replied, chuffing out another aggravated breath, "and yet you're calling us now, so I assume you're ready for us to bring you your rig?"

"Not yet, but quite soon. Is it stocked as I requested?"

"The floor of your trailer is covered in those reusable shopping bags you requested."

"Excellent! However, rather than you bringing my car and trailer to me where I am at present, it will be safer if we meet elsewhere."

"When and where?"

"I am getting to it. I have acquired a secure location for the summer, but I cannot check in right away, so the issue is timing. I could leave here tomorrow, except I am not quite finished with my PT. More importantly, I would end up bouncing around from place to place during those weeks leading up to my check-in, and I would rather not leave such a trail."

"You're saying you're better off where you are, that your jump to your secure summer location should take no longer than absolutely necessary?"

"That is it precisely. Unless something happens to force me to flee this location sooner, I suggest you meet me the week before Memorial Day, one of you driving my rig, the other following in one of your own vehicles."

Grayson said, "We can do that."

"Very good. And should you receive a cryptic text from an unknown number, it would signal that I had to leave my present abode *immediately* and that I will meet you at our designated location within a twenty-four-hour window."

Grayson scoffed. "What, are we playing spy games now?"

"My precautions are warranted, Grayson. My contact at the FBI let me know she found a leak in her division. She was supposed to get back to me when the threat was resolved, yet I have not heard from her since."

Grayson and Alberto spoke as one. "Your contact *where*?"

"You didn't think me foolish enough to take on the Lucchese Family on my own, did you?" When silence on their end of the call lingered, she sighed.

"Unbelievable."

"Hey, that's *our* line," Alberto grumbled.

She ignored the dig. "Gentlemen, I propose we meet at noon in Las Vegas in the parking lot of the Walmart on East Tropicana *exactly two weeks from today*, so that I can drive directly to my next location. That date will change only if you receive a text from me signaling that I have been forced to leave immediately. Should you receive such a text, we will meet at the same place, same time of day, but within the next twenty-four hours."

"Where in the parking lot?"

"It matters not; I will find you. We will switch vehicles and depart immediately without speaking to each other. I will leave instructions on the front seat of the car I am driving, telling you where you are to return the car, after which you will return home in your own vehicle. Of course, I will reimburse you personally for your time and expenses."

"Wait. *Depart without speaking to each other?*"

She thought Alberto sounded livid. *Curious.*

"Why, yes. It will be safer—"

"Yeah, that's a no-go for me too," Grayson agreed. "There has to be a quiet restaurant nearby where we could have lunch and a discreet conversation."

Miss Finch sighed again. "Well, perhaps."

"Well, *perhaps* we won't hand over your keys until we've sat and talked," Alberto growled, piling on.

"Nicely played, 'Berto," Grayson laughed.

Miss Finch sighed a third time. "Merciful heavens. I declare you two are worse than Hugo and Pouncer when they are in cahoots."

"Hugo and Pouncer? Yeah, *and* we get to pet Hugo and Pouncer," Alberto demanded.

"Well, Hugo, at any rate," Grayson amended.

"Point taken," Alberto replied. "We want to pet Hugo. We'll *wave* to Pouncer. From a distance."

"Pouncer will be quite disappointed in you two," Miss Finch sniffed.

Alberto scoffed. "Yeah? Well, I ain't chancing a trip to Urgent Care."

———— ● ————

THE WATCHING AND waiting through the remainder of the week rubbed on Miss Finch like coarse sandpaper. Nerves on edge, she often startled at unexpected noises until Pouncer yowled and Hugo's nose nudged her hand while he turned sad, concerned eyes on her.

"Sorry, my darlings. I am not behaving well, am I?"

She turned her heart toward the One who is sure and true.

Lord God, you have never failed me. I trust you. Yes, I truly do—so please help me master my fears. Yet, even as I rest in you, would you kindly warn me if Don Massimo's hired trackers are closing in? Thank you.

Right now, I again receive your peace. I declare that I will not fret because I trust in you.

———————— ● ————————

TWO DAYS LATER, while leaving the beach parking lot, she dug in her bag and powered on the burner she used for Agent Claussen. She nearly backed over a curb when a recording announced, "You have one new message."

She braked, calmed herself, and listened. The voicemail went straight to a brief, stiffly worded message.

"We identified our division's suspected leaker a week ago and have been monitoring the agent and her communications. Today, she *and* a coworker did not return from lunch and neither of them is answering their cells. Although we kept your last-tracked location a closely held secret, this dual defection makes us suspect our division is more compromised than we thought. The second individual AWOL has access to classified satellite feeds and their backup tapes and has been viewing them for several days. They must have found what they were looking for because a scan of the leaker's phone logs shows a call to an unregistered phone in LA *last evening*. Bottom line? We strongly recommend you either report to your nearest FBI field office or, if you insist on managing your own security, *move ASAP*."

A pause followed, then, "I am truly sorry. You were right."

Miss Finch listened to the message again, then powered the phone off. "I need to go," she whispered. "The question is, has my house been pinpointed? Dare I return to it to gather a few additional items?"

Halfway up her street, she passed a car she'd never seen before. Without slowing or turning her head, she continued on, drove around the corner, then wound her way back through several side streets, and used an alley to study the unfamiliar car.

She pulled her binoculars from her beach bag and focused them on the man sitting in the car's driver's seat. As the man's face came into focus, shock rippled through her body.

I know him. He's a PI from Los Angeles.

She sorted through her mental rolodex of Los Angeles detectives, finally coming up with the man's name . . . and his less-than-stellar reputation.

Thank you, Lord. Thank you for showing him to me.

Turning toward the back seat, she whispered, "Time to go, my sweet lovelies."

———— ❖ ————

SHE BACKED SLOWLY out of the alley, rolled into the street, and drove off, her mind fixed on the details and tasks ahead of her. She was well on her way out of town, headed north on I-15, when she made her first call.

"Myra, Gladys here."

Myra was instantly alert. "Yes, Gladys?"

"I am afraid I must cut short my stay and cancel my upcoming appointments at the clinic. I also recommend *not* sending cleaners to tidy up the house for at least a week."

After a short hesitation, Myra answered, "I understand. Will there be anything of value left in the house?"

"Nothing I cannot live without. I carry what I absolutely need with me at all times. Feel free to distribute whatever can be used and toss the rest."

"And the car?"

"I estimate it will be left in the clinic parking lot, keys under the front seat, no later than day after tomorrow."

Myra asked in a whisper, "Will you be all right?"

"Thank you for asking, Myra. I am confident in this one thing: I am held in God's mighty hand, and nothing and no one can snatch me from him."

"I admire your conviction, Gladys."

"And I thank you for your unstinting help when I was in need, Myra. My payment and the donation I promised will be forthcoming from an account you do not recognize. The Lord bless you."

She drove until she spotted a relatively safe-looking gas station and mini mart. She pulled up to the pump. Before she got out, she dug around in her go bag and retrieved the burner she used to call Grayson. She pressed the power button and prayed while she waited for it to power up. Nodding to herself, she keyed in a short text.

Starting my summer vacation tomorrow

———— ❖ ————

ONE OF THE LEAKERS in Claussen's department had access to classified satellite feeds and their backup tapes? The very idea made Miss Finch's skin itch as she took the I-215 cutoff to avoid going through more of Los Angeles on her way to Vegas. Instead, she traversed the outskirts of the city and reconnected with I-15 north of the city proper. Hugo and Pouncer slept peacefully in their seats, but Miss Finch kept her eyes roving continually, scouting out danger before she drove into it.

It was late evening when she reached Vegas. She chose a three-star casino hotel on Tropicana, let Hugo and Pouncer do their business in the casino's pet park, then checked in, paying with a credit card from her family's trust . . . a fund that did not bear her name. She put Hugo and Pouncer into their carrier and rolled them up to the hotel's check-in counter.

"Two hundred dollar pet fee, refundable if there's no damage," the bored clerk muttered.

"I understand."

"Restaurant open 24/7."

"Thank you."

Late that night, she lay in bed trying to sleep, yet her busy mind would not shut down. Finally, she climbed out and knelt by her bed.

"Lord God, I place my whole self in your hands. I believe you led me to expose Don Massimo and his son's crimes, their 'murder by accident' schemes, some of which were convenient means of disposing of enemies, but others . . . possibly murder for hire.

"By opening Don Massimo to deep federal investigation, I pray his older, deeper sins will come to light. This is my hope, Lord, that you would bring justice to bear, justice for . . . my family.

"And because I believe you have led me this way, I can trust you to see me safely through every danger before me. I need not fret. Even should I lose my life, I trust in you. My future is secure in your hands. Amen."

———— ❖ ————

AT NOON THE NEXT day, she met Grayson and Alberto at the nearby Walmart. She was, she admitted to herself, very glad to see them both.

After a quick lunch, Alberto drove away in her borrowed car, and Grayson followed in his own automobile.

She settled Hugo and Pouncer into the woody's back seat and left soon after . . . but she did not go far. Instead, she checked into a crowded, unremarkable RV park just north of Las Vegas.

I will stay here, watching carefully, until I am reasonably certain I am not being followed. No sense my being in a hurry to 'get out of Dodge' if I'm being tracked every mile I travel.

AFTER STAYING TWO more nights in Vegas to make certain she was not being followed, she drove farther north, knowing she had one more week to kill. Sadly, she realized that her lovingly restored classic car was her worst enemy, attracting unwanted attention everywhere she went. Because of this, she traveled back roads and dry camped in sketchy pullouts or primitive roadside campgrounds, while making her way to the area north of Lake Tahoe.

Since it was still spring and cold in the mountains, she did not need to compete for places to rest for a night or two. The supplies Grayson and Alberto purchased and loaded into her trailer meant her only necessary stops were to gas her car. Otherwise, she kept to herself, parked for the night after dark wherever she could, staying a second night only if she was alone, or leaving early the next day if she was not, speaking to as few people as possible.

Praying God would make her invisible to her enemies.

THE INDIVIDUAL FOLLOWING her was, however, patient and had no intention of confronting or harming her . . . at this time. That fun would come later. For now, it was enough to trail along after the unsuspecting woman until she settled in.

After all, in the game of cat and mouse, the pleasure was found in *playing* with one's prey.

POSTSCRIPT

FINALLY, ON WEDNESDAY morning, the week before Memorial Day, Miss Finch pointed her car down the west shore of Lake Tahoe. She drove south along the lake's long length, then ascended Emerald Bay Road. She followed that road high above Emerald Bay itself until she passed Inspiration Point, then descended slowly, taking care on the hairpin curves.

Not much farther, a few miles before reaching the town of South Lake Tahoe, she spied her turnoff. She headed south again and wended her way up the road until she spotted signage hanging over a freshly graveled lane on her right.

Before she started down that road, she sighed with relief and slowed to study the words arching high overhead.

BRIGHT STAR
SUMMER RV RESIDENCE
PRIVATE PROPERTY
Visitors Must Check In at Office

"Hugo, Pouncer? We have made it," she whispered. "Thank you, Lord God, for seeing us safely here."

She drove on until she reached, on her right, the rustic-looking cabin that served as Bright Star's office. She came to a stop just short of the office at the same time a man and a teen were wrestling what appeared to be a heavy laundry bin over the office door's threshold and onto the porch.

The man, wearing a Bright Star work shirt, glanced up, spotted her car, and stopped cold. He gawked at her car—like people everywhere did.

He stepped off the porch to ogle the car up close.

"*Wow*," he muttered under his breath.

Don't you dare put your fingerprints on my car, Miss Finch growled to herself, climbing out of the driver's seat to walk around to the office.

The teen, wearing a Bright Star polo, joined the man as he examined her car's hood. "What kinda car *is* this?"

"This, my boy, is a 1950 Ford Custom Country Squire—a panel wagon commonly known as a 'woody.'"

The kid echoed the man's sentiments. "Er, *wow*."

She cleared her throat. "1951, actually."

The man tore his eyes from the car and stared around, looking for her. "Down here," Miss Finch murmured.

THE END

But what's next?

Read on and enjoy the first two chapters of
The Tahoe Mysteries, Book 1:
Number 1 with a Bullet

PREPARE YOURSELF FOR

The TAHOE MYSTERIES

Book 1: *Number 1 with a Bullet*
Book 2: *Be Quick or Be Dead*
Book 3: *Death on the Big Blue*, 2026
and
Murder by Accident, A Miss Finch Prequel

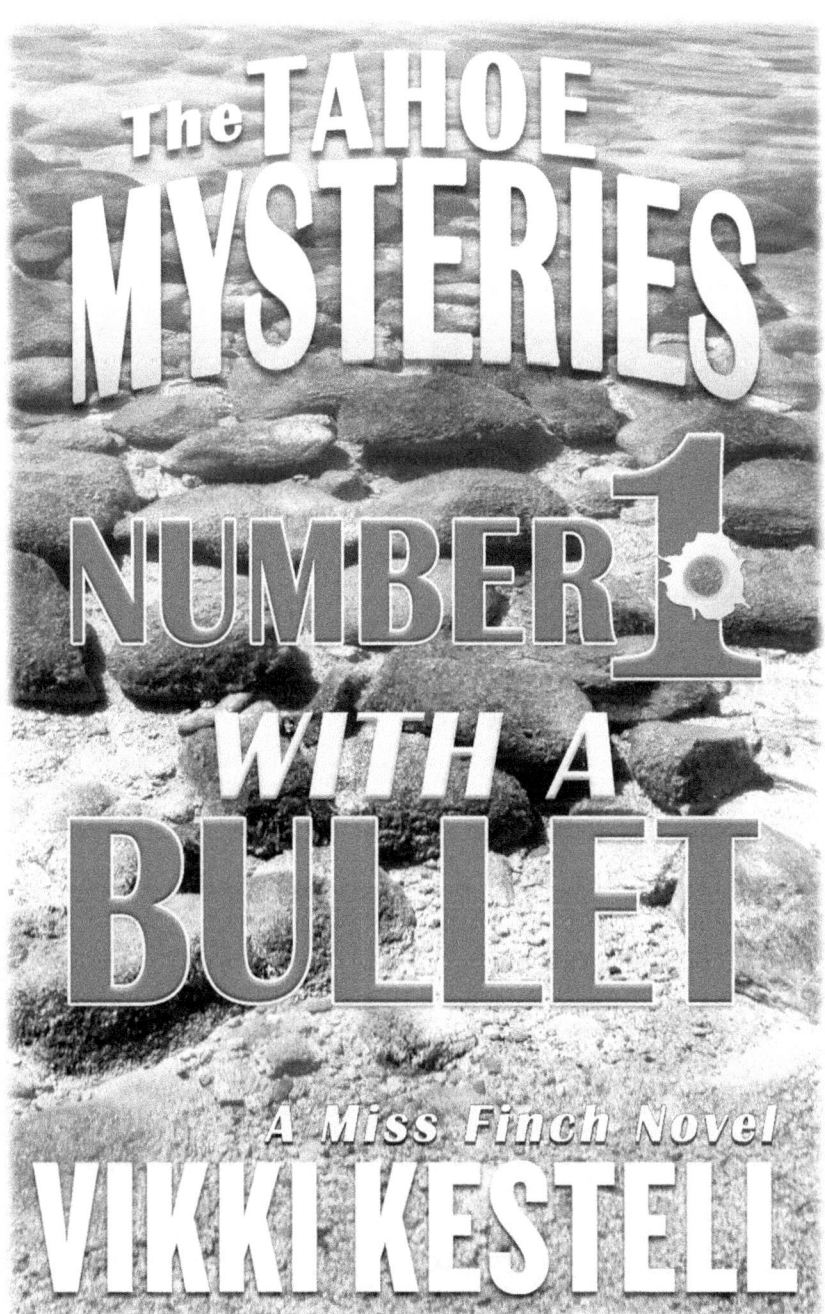

The TAHOE MYSTERIES

NUMBER 1

WITH A BULLET

A Miss Finch Novel

VIKKI KESTELL

Faith-Filled Fiction™

www.faith-filledfiction.com | www.vikkikestell.com

CHAPTER 1

BRIGHT STAR SUMMER RV RESIDENCE, SOUTH END OF LAKE TAHOE

WEDNESDAY PRIOR TO MEMORIAL DAY, MAY 21

SIMON FLETCHER TURNED right off the paved road and drove his pickup around to the back side of the refurbished log cabin that served as his employer's office. He parked, then strode to the front side of the cabin, stepped out onto the road and faced the park's entrance, just beyond the office. He pressed the button on the remote in his pocket and watched Bright Star's bronze gates slide apart.

With chin tucked and arms folded across his chest, Bright Star's Facilities and Security Manager glared through the open entrance with the intensity of a Marine drill instructor inspecting a ragged row of raw recruits at oh four thirty in the dark a.m.—which was exactly how Simon viewed his Bright Star responsibilities: His purpose was to shape, shine, mold, cajole, or pummel the pieces and parts of Bright Star residing under his purview until each one exceeded his expectations.

Barely topping five feet nine but wide and muscled across the chest, Simon was a rock of a man, a machine unacquainted with the word "quit." From his strong physical presence to a "get it done" work ethic, Simon's every action oozed purpose. No detail escaped him, nor did he tolerate much in the way of nonsense.

Simon's fellow Marine MPs had laughingly referred to him as the Corps' human armored fighting vehicle. They'd nod sagely, and in the same way they might say, "We need an M1 Abrams to bust through that concrete barrier," they would shout, "This drunken brawl requires our resident tank: Call in the Fletcher!"

They weren't far off the mark. Simon Fletcher was, more often than not, inclined to roll over or through any impediment foolish enough to plant itself between him and his objective.

Feeling a familiar anger rising, he sniffed and reminded himself, *The Corps is in your rearview mirror, Fletcher. All twenty years of it. Nothing for you there, so stop looking back.*

A snide voice replied, *Once a Marine, always a Marine, Fletch. Semper fi.* "Yeah, yeah."

Whatever.

Simon had prided himself on his accomplishments in the Corps, but now two years out from his discharge, he no longer thought of himself as anything special. Near the end of his second year of civilian life, he considered himself an average guy with sandy hair, light brown eyes, and bland features capped by a nose that had been broken twice, set once.

At forty-eight years of age, he had nothing to show for his years in the Corps—no career, wife, kids, or living relations. As far as Simon was concerned, the family he'd chosen and poured his life's blood into had turned its back on him.

His years in the Marines aside, in this last year he had become a valued worker and a steady, faithful partner to Joe and Holly Mitchell, Bright Star's owners. He was helpful and friendly with people, too—with the exception of the aforementioned "foolish impediment" type. And rarely did friend or acquaintance of any length call him by his given name, Simon. Sooner or later, everyone fell into using his last name, Fletcher, or its shortened version, "Fletch."

Backlit by the early morning sun, Simon stood before Bright Star's open gate and mentally gauged the park's readiness to receive its first residents. Residents who would begin arriving midday tomorrow.

He tried to put himself in their shoes: *If I were an incoming guest, what would catch my eye as I arrived?*

The gate itself was as beautiful as it was imposing, a splendid work of hardened steel and metal sculpture. Custom-designed and built for the park, the gate featured Bright Star's bronzed logo. Holly Mitchell generally kept the gate open during the day while she staffed the office but closed and locked outside of office hours. The automated gate retracted when residents entered their personal code on the gate's keypad. A Bright Star employee could also open or close the gate by pressing a button inside the office or on a remote such as the one Simon held.

Of course, Holly had requested certain features to protect the privacy of Bright Star's residents. To satisfy her, Simon had posted prominent signage several yards before the gate. In flowing gold letters, the sign declared,

BRIGHT STAR SUMMER RV RESIDENCE
PRIVATE PROPERTY
Visitors Must Check In at Office

Simon thought Holly had exhibited a bit of paranoia when she insisted Bright Star's gate be "extra strong so our residents feel safe," but she wrote the checks. After Simon finished his work with the fabricators, the installed gate could withstand the impact of a half-ton pickup truck—as could the tall steel fence set in concrete extending twenty-five feet from the gate on both sides, the fence's two ends vanishing into forest shrubbery.

Holly had actually lobbied for fencing the entire park, but her husband, Joe, had put his foot down.

"We're trying to give our guests a piece of the great outdoors, Hol," Joe had protested, "not a prison cell. Besides, we can't afford such an expense."

Joe's reaction didn't keep Holly from assigning Simon the task of installing a four-camera video surveillance system to capture video of the road leading up to Bright Star's gate. Over Bright Star's private road, from where it joined the main road, stood an arched sign displaying Bright Star's bronzed logo and smaller words declaring, "Office Ahead." Simon had mounted the first camera there, capturing images of all vehicles that turned in. He located the second and third cameras along the half-mile stretch of road leading to the office, and a final camera at the gate. A monitor on the office counter displayed the video feed, cycling through the four camera views every few seconds.

The gate and cameras couldn't guarantee the residents' security, but they went a long way toward projecting the perception of privacy.

Speaking of privacy . . .

Simon walked through the open entrance. A broad swath of freshly laid and striped asphalt scribed a graceful, elongated circuit from the gate, through the park's forest and past all the RV sites, and returning to the gate. Simon knew every twist and turn of that wide, one-way loop like the back of his own hand, just like he knew every inch of Bright Star's thirty acres. He'd spent the last nine months hard at work alongside Joe and Holly, helping them bring their dream of a unique summer RV park to birth.

"One ritzy, glorified campground," he muttered under his breath.

The park was much more, although Simon wouldn't admit it to just anyone. Fact was, he was proud of Bright Star and its unique flavor.

Twenty-four pristine RV sites poked their long double driveways into the park's perimeter loop like so many spokes on a very out-of-round wheel. Each RV site, in addition to being set far back from the road, was shaded by a canopy of tall pines and endowed with a full RV hookup (including cable and internet), a sizeable patch of perfectly edged grass, and a tidy paved patio area complete with firepit, picnic table, and chilled drinking water dispenser. Every site's driveway also provided a level pad for its resident's RV and ample parking for the resident's vehicles. The kicker? Forty feet or more of natural mountain verdure separated the sites one from another, effectively achieving the impression of peaceful mountain solitude for the occupants of each site.

Simon shifted his internal gaze. Yes, the RV sites were impressive, and pictures of the various sites on Bright Star's website had done them justice. Still, it was the architectural renderings of the large "island" built up in the center of the park that clinched the deal for most prospective residents.

The island's tapered promontory jutted toward the park entrance, commanding the attention of all comers—as it was designed to do. Four ascending tiers climbed the promontory and were crowned with banks of concealed water jets. From those jets, sprays of water leapt, twirled, and pirouetted in mesmerizing cadence to soft music, while hidden lights infused the spurts and feathery showers with intense color.

Or at least they did in the fountain designer's colorful animation.

Simon smiled to himself. *Can't wait to see them in action again.*

The promontory with its terraces of gamboling water dancers was the taste that tantalized, the crooked finger that beckoned visitors into the park and onward toward the island's further attractions . . . and said further attractions did not disappoint.

Next, the island showcased a splendid though modest-sized swimming complex. The complex's main pool, closest to the dancing water feature, had a large three-to-five-foot-deep section dedicated to family fun. The deck on one side sported two water slides. On the far end of the family pool was a twelve-foot "deep end" reserved for a single spring board and two diving platforms of varying heights.

Residents could also enjoy an adult-only lap pool with three warmed swim lanes, each forty feet in length. A six-foot wall separated the family pool from the swim lanes, reducing the noise coming from the family pools for those wanting to enjoy a more sedate swim time.

Within the swimming complex's main enclosure, residents and their guests would also find two hot tubs, three lounging areas, a half dozen shaded patio tables, and two exquisitely appointed restrooms for showering and changing into or out of swim wear.

Lastly, the complex boasted a zero-to-ten-inch-deep wading and spray pool for toddlers, complete with tiny water slide, close parental seating, and its own restrooms. The kiddie section sat within a separate enclosure, unattached to the rest of the swimming complex, for safety reasons.

Aside from the dancing water feature, the swimming complex was Bright Star's definitive jewel and leading attraction.

"But wait! There's more," Simon snickered.

Down the island from those appealing amenities, atop a picture-perfect lawn, awaited a barbecue zone, furnished with gas grills and shaded picnic tables for the residents' pleasure. Farther across the grass was an inviting group firepit encircled by log seating. On the grass beyond the firepit stood a volleyball *slash* badminton net, and beyond the net, a fenced pickleball court.

A large cabin at the farthest end of the island served as an indoor rec facility. One side of the rec facility was dedicated to group events and included a community kitchen and dining room. The other half of the building was split between a small gym equipped with weights, cardio machines, mats for stretching, and a game room stocked with board games, puzzles, and video game consoles. A low structure off to the side of the rec facility bore the sign, "Bright Star Resident Laundry Facility."

The amenities on the island were interconnected by broad paths of local stone and mortar. Simon and his boss, Joe, had painstakingly laid every foot of those paths. Given that the majority of their clientele were likely to be retirees, Simon and Joe had made certain the path surfaces were flat and smooth with nary a single trip hazard, while solar lighting along the paths ensured easy navigation after dark.

Simon nodded to himself. The park's features and facilities had that "brand-new" sparkle to them because they were, in fact, brand-new. Furthermore, every aspect of the park shouted "select," "private," and "discriminating"—which was the whole point.

Bright Star was the only Tahoe RV park to bill itself as a summer *residence*. One did not stay overnight at Bright Star or check in one week and check out the next. No, in this RV park, guests paid handsomely (and in advance) to call Bright Star their home away from home for the entire season, Memorial Day weekend through Labor Day.

Twenty-three candidates had flocked to Bright Star's website and each shelled out thirty-six grand, the equivalent of twelve thousand dollars a month, to spend the summer at Bright Star. The last berth to be booked at Bright Star—a worry that had plagued Holly—had finally been filled just two weeks ago.

"And we're almost ready for them," Simon murmured, "although it's a mighty big 'almost.'"

Half of Simon's job as Bright Star's facilities and security manager was to maintain the island and its amenities in its "brand-new" state. With the exception of one essential element, all features were up and operational, inspected, approved, and certified where required. But the "one essential element," the single impediment facing Simon before Bright Star's grand opening?

"The swimming complex's blasted water pump," he growled.

Simon needed the pump that fed and cycled water to the dancing water feature and the several pools, and he needed it *today*. The original pump, a large and complex piece of hardware, electronics, and accompanying software, ordered six months in advance, had functioned perfectly.

Until it didn't.

The fountains had danced and twirled to Holly, Joe, and Simon's shared delight. But an hour into the pump's trial performance, it failed and died.

Simon's call to Bright Star's Vegas supplier—after he had recited the pump's serial number to the supplier and he had checked the manufacturer's website—revealed that Bright Star's pump was subject to a national recall. The problem was a fabricating defect resulting in faulty chips on the pump's motherboard. Worse, the recall had depleted the manufacturer's warehouse of that model, meaning Bright Star's pump was now out of stock.

As it turned out, *thanks be to God*, their supplier had an extra pump of the desired model on their shelves. Joe had reeled Holly down from the office ceiling, and the freight company had delivered Bright Star's replacement pump two weeks ago.

Except . . .

Except the crated pump had arrived looking like it had fallen off the truck somewhere between Vegas and Tahoe, bounced down the highway, endured a glancing encounter with a semi, and cartwheeled onto the shoulder . . . where it was scraped off the road, returned to the truck, and delivered to Bright Star with a smarmy smile and an affable but disingenuous "sign here, please."

As Simon recalled the delivery guy's false warmth, a scowl traversed his weathered face, a scowl that could have melted the bronzed Bright Star logo right off the entrance gate. Simon clenched his teeth. He wasn't a cursing kind of guy, but after twenty years in the Corps, he'd become acquainted with every swear word known to the English language, along with a smattering of Spanish ones. He may not have uttered those curse words aloud; nonetheless, his personal convictions didn't keep those words from popping into his head during trying situations where they'd pound on the door of his mind, hoping to wear him down, trying to make their way into the open air.

"Nope. Get lost," he growled aloud, waggling his tense shoulders. "I don't use the mouth with which I praise God to also utter obscenities. Beat it!"

Simon had refused to sign for the pump and told the driver to wait while he photographed the moose-sized crate (crushed on two sides, caved in on another) to document the exterior damage. While the driver protested the delay, Simon tried to swivel the crate into the light to get a better shot. The driver shut his mouth and found something else to do when loose bits of the shattered pump fell from a crack in the crate onto the truck's floor.

"Good grief," Simon had muttered. He took pictures of the broken bits and sent all the photos via email to the supplier in Las Vegas, then followed up with a phone call to the supplier's office.

"I've declined delivery of the pump," Simon told him. "Check your inbox for the details."

After reviewing Simon's photos, the man on the other end of the call was suitably apologetic. "I don't blame you. Look, I'm sorry this happened, and I'll lambast the freight company. Unfortunately and like I told you earlier, that particular pump is in high demand across the casino industry to run their water features, and thus is on back order. You can thank your lucky stars, though, because I have one of those pumps coming in later this month. I can have it to you . . . one sec."

I don't thank stars, lucky or otherwise, Simon had declared silently. *God, are you listening? I really need you right now. Please help.*

He heard the clicking of a mouse as the man searched his inventory.

"Earliest I can get it to you is late Tuesday."

"Really? *This* Tuesday?"

"Nope, sorry. I meant the Tuesday before Memorial Day, about two weeks from now."

"Outstanding," Simon had muttered under his breath. Then, admitting they would at least have a working pump before Bright Star's opening day, he added a heartfelt, *Thank you, Lord!*

Unless something else had gone wrong, the supplier should have delivered the pump as promised late yesterday afternoon. Simon would have personally checked the delivery when it arrived, but he'd had to leave work early for an urgent root canal. With the pump's arrival, Simon's sole priority as he clocked into work this morning, the Wednesday prior to Memorial Day weekend, was to install said pump, connect the various elements of the fountain and swimming complex's plumbing to the pump, update the pump's automation software on the swimming complex's laptop, and put the system back to work.

With the pump system up and operational, Simon would be able to fill the several pools, cycle the water and chemicals through the entire system and, *finally*, test the water to meet the Health Department's commercial pool requirements.

It irked Simon that today was supposed to have been his first day off in three weeks. He needed the brief respite after months of concentrated effort. It was supposed to have been a peaceful pause before Lake Tahoe's summer insanity officially kicked off.

"But nooo," he groused. "Instead of a well-deserved day off, Bright Star's swimming complex is giving *me* a complex—not to mention, now that the numbing for my root canal is wearing off, my jaw feels like it was kicked by a mule."

At present, the fountains, pools, and hot tubs were dry as dust. And until the pumping system was online, Bright Star's "jewel" would remain sadly lusterless.

Simon muttered a line he knew by heart: "Filling those pools could take up to eighteen hours. Nevertheless, God willing, I *will* get it done and the complex *will* open on time. *Oorah.*"

Simon turned and walked back toward the front of Bright Star's office. About the same time, Holly Mitchell burst from the cabin's doorway, the screen door slapping closed behind her. They met on the grass between the office and the road.

Holly was in her early fifties, a redhead trending toward gray. She was pleasant enough to work for—unless she was disturbed or anxious—and one look told Simon that Holly was totally rocking her disturbed and anxious alter ego. Her fading red curls trembled, and she clenched and unclenched her hands as she spoke.

"Fletcher, you have no idea how glad I am to see you! We have a bit of an emergency here, and I need your help."

Simon wasn't all that surprised. Working with Joe was great—he took problems in stride. But working for Holly followed a pattern: New day? New crisis.

"Nothing's on fire. Don't see any residents queuing up ahead of their move-in date. What's the big emergency?"

Besides our problem child of a swimming complex? Please don't go there, Holly. My stress meter is pegged out without you standing on it too.

Holly went there.

"Well, *the pools*, of course! The replacement pump arrived last evening, but can you believe this? The supplier sent *the wrong one!* Of course, the delivery guy just shrugged. As soon as Joe realized it was the wrong model, he called the supplier, after which he jumped in his truck and headed for Vegas to get the right one. The supplier promised to have it ready to load into Joe's truck first thing today.

"Joe drove through the night until he got to Vegas, then slept in his truck in the supplier's parking lot until the sun came up. He called a few minutes ago to say he's catching some breakfast and will be waiting at the supplier's door when they open this morning. He'll head back as soon as they load the *right* pump onto the bed of his truck."

She licked her lips. "Fletch, if the pool isn't filled by tomorrow, midday, the five residents scheduled to check in every hour from noon forward will not be merely disappointed. Oh, *no*, not simply 'put out.' They will be disgruntled, Simon, *disgruntled!* And you know how disgruntled people love to post negative reviews online! One couple, the Gormans, are bringing their granddaughters to Tahoe for the holiday weekend, and our swimming complex, in particular, figures high in their plans. *High*, Fletch!"

Simon stifled a yawn as Holly droned on. *Need. More. Coffee.*

"We don't dare launch our inaugural season on a sour note, Fletch, not after the way we've promoted Bright Star's grand opening. The residents' leases state that if they find substantive fault with Bright Star's advertised accommodations or amenities, they have five days to request a full refund. Fletch, we *can't afford* to refund any of our reservations. We need that money to pay you and operate the park through the summer season and-and-and to support Joe and me during the offseason."

The thirty acres Bright Star sat on, approximately halfway between Mount Tallac Trail and Fallen Leaf Lake, had originally belonged to Joe's grandparents and had been used in decades past as a summer camp, complete with horses and stables. Under a local zoning "grandfather" clause, long-term use of the land as a summer camp had afforded the Mitchells significant leeway in how they could renovate and utilize the property going forward.

Consequently, when Joe Mitchell inherited his grandfather's Tahoe property, he and Holly had retired early from their San Diego real estate business and moved to the modest cabin Joe's grandparents had lived in. Over the sixteen months since then, they had sunk their life savings and the profits from the sale of their company—plus a hefty mortgage—into turning a dated summer camp into a luxury RV paradise. It was no big secret to Simon that Joe and Holly's financial future depended on Bright Star being a success.

The nearer opening day loomed, the more anxious Holly became. And when Holly tensed up? She tended to micromanage.

Simon unfolded his arms. "Yeah, yeah. No pump, no pool, no *bueno*. I get it, Hol. Don't sweat it; when Joe gets here, I'll jump on the installation and get the pools filled on time. When do you expect him back?"

"He should be here late this afternoon, but with Joe out on the road, that leaves us shorthanded. I need you to take on Joe's tasks today, Fletch. Of course, the minute he gets here, you can switch to the pump install."

"Roger. Do all of Joe's chores, then install the pump when he gets here with it. Any specific issues I should know about?"

Holly hedged. "Well, there's Skipper."

Skipper Mitchell, Joe and Holly's fourteen-year-old nephew, had been with them an entire week, but it hadn't required the full seven days to convince the three of them that the kid was a right royal pain.

"What's he done this time?"

"Nothing, but that's just it. He won't do anything. I can't get him to unlock his bedroom door, let alone get him started on his chores, and I'm depending on him today. Especially today."

She shook her head. "I don't know if I can abide that boy through the entire summer, Fletch. I simply cannot tolerate the level of . . . disorder that follows him around."

Simon snorted. Skipper was under a form of house arrest as the condition of his probation. To complicate matters, Kathy, the boy's mother and the Mitchells' sister-in-law—*former* sister-in-law—could not miss work while Skipper was on probation without risking her job. So, at her request and with Joe and Holly's agreement, the judge overseeing Skipper's case had sentenced the boy to a summer of labor under his uncle and aunt's supervision. The alternative would have left Skipper alone at home through the summer, wearing an ankle monitor, but without structure or supervision, while his mother worked.

A recipe for further trouble if I've ever seen one, Simon thought. *The odds of that kid making it through the summer without breaking the conditions of his probation? Pretty much nonexistent.*

A year ago, to the Mitchells' dismay, Skipper's dad, Pete—Joe's much younger brother—had bailed on his family. He'd disappeared and his whereabouts remained unknown, which left his wife to support and raise their son on her own.

Now Skipper is a ticking time bomb, pushing the envelope hard, finding new ways to express his anger daily. Not unlike a few pimple-faced Marine recruits I've encountered over the years who were given the choice: join up or go to jail.

And what a ball of fun they were when out on their first leave as a Marine. Full of themselves and looking for trouble.

"I was hoping you would talk to him, Fletch. After all, he'll be working for you once we open."

Simon rubbed the back of his neck. "Talking isn't likely to put things right in that boy. The kid needs routine, physically demanding labor, and a firm hand. Someone to help him learn personal accountability."

"You fit the bill perfectly, Fletch, which is why I'm asking for your help. For example, he was supposed to help Joe hang the residents' site banners today."

A wrought iron pole with a perpendicular side arm stood at the head of each resident's double driveway. The pole's side arm was designed to display a vertical flag easily seen from the road. Holly had made the twenty-four colorful banners herself, adding to each one a site number and the residents' last name in applique. She was justifiably proud of the welcoming touch the banners would provide.

Simon shook his head. "Look, I'm a military cop by training, not a nursemaid, Holly. My style would be to bust open the kid's door, flip over his bed, and dump him onto the floor. But I'm not an MP any longer and he's not a Marine recruit. I'm not going to roust that spoiled kid from bed if he's too lazy to get up."

Holly's eyes glistened. "Please, Fletch?"

Well, crud.

Simon blew out a long breath. "Can't promise it will improve his sorry attitude, but I'll at least get him moving today. Now, is that everything?"

Holly fidgeted. "Just one more . . . item." She glanced through Bright Star's entrance and down the road to the right where Site 1 was tucked into the trees, its driveway not even visible from the gate. "Our first resident arrives today."

Simon's jaw about hit the floor. "Are you kidding me, Holly? Today is Wednesday. Residents aren't supposed to start checking in until tomorrow, noon. Those are *your* rules—no one checks in before the Thursday preceding Memorial Day weekend. No. One."

Fixing her eyes on the grass, Holly toed the broad leaves of a budding dandelion. "This isn't on me, Fletch. Joe made some kind of special exception for this woman, and he didn't even consult me! Of course I knew she was registered, but then yesterday Joe announced that, for some reason, she needs to check in a day early. Because he owes her some sort of a big favor, he made the exception."

Simon's brows drew together. "What kind of favor?"

"I have no idea, and believe me, I've asked. But whenever I've tried to put the question to Joe, he clams up like it's a big, dark secret or something. Anyway, this woman asked specifically for Site 1 because it backs up to the creek. Joe told me she studied the park's layout online and apparently likes the sound of a babbling brook nearby."

Simon made a disgusted noise. "And she's checking in today? Good grief! Like we don't have enough going on. Fine. We'll figure it out. What time is she due?"

"Joe said about 11:00." Then she looked up and skewered Simon with her gaze. "I need you to park her RV, Fletch."

Crud and double crud.

Bright Star rules dictated that only designated Bright Star employees were allowed to position and park resident RVs. Joe was an absolute savant at backing up the type and size of luxury RV Bright Star's residents were expected to bring. Simon was no slouch at the task, but he didn't have the artistry or flair Joe did. And the bigger the RV, the less confident Simon felt.

"What's this woman driving or hauling?"

Holly's mouth tightened. "And that's another thing, Fletcher. Bright Star is an *exclusive* summer residence. Do you know how stringent our require-ments must be for us to actualize and model that exclusive status?"

Simon did know, and he quickly nodded his head hoping she'd skip over the lecture. Nope. Nothing could deter Holly from reiterating those stringent requirements aloud as though he'd never heard them.

She ticked them off on her fingers. "Resident RVs must be a minimum of thirty feet in length.

"Resident RVs must be no older than seven years.

"Resident RVs must be clean and well maintained with no noticeable neglect, damage, missing parts, or discoloration to the frame or paint.

"Resident RVs must be leveled and skirted within 24 hours of arrival.

"Resident RV systems must be compatible with and connected to Bright Star's electrical, water, and septic systems within 24 hours of arrival and during the entirety of the residency period.

"Residents must maintain their RV and assigned site in a manner that reflects and honors the spirit of Bright Star Summer RV Residence—with the exception of their site's lawn, of course. The sprinklers will water it, and Joe will mow the grass weekly."

"So what's the problem? If she signed the lease, she agreed to the terms."

Holly fidgeted and dug her shoe into the doomed dandelion. "Joe said . . ."

"Joe said what?"

With a huff, Holly muttered, "Joe said he'd made two concessions for this-this-this *woman*, this *Miss Finch*."

"Miss Finch, huh? And, pray tell, what two concessions did Joe make on this mysterious woman's behalf?"

"Don't tease me, Simon Fletcher! This is not a subject to make light of."

"Sure, Holly. What allowances did Joe extend to the woman?"

"Well, the first was allowing her to check in a day early. He would not elaborate on the second, but he said . . . he *promised* me that it would not lower Bright Star's standards."

Simon looked aside. "Interesting."

"*Not* interesting. Annoying. Maddening. And-and-and *wrong!*"

Simon slid a hand across his mouth to smother the laugh threatening to jump out. Holly was nothing if not melodramatic concerning her precious standards.

An inappropriate display of humor successfully averted, Simon suggested, "Why don't we wait until this Miss Finch arrives before we worry about how her rig might impact Bright Star? In the meantime, I'll attempt to get Skipper moving so he and I can get the site banners hung."

Holly nodded her agreement. "Thank you, Fletcher."

———————◆———————

SIMON LEFT THE OFFICE, glancing at the sign in the door's window that read, "Bright Star Office Hours, Monday-Saturday, 9:00 a.m. to 5:00 p.m.; Sundays, 1:00 to 5:00 p.m." He grabbed the keys to one of the park's two service vehicles—small, fuel-efficient pickups emblazoned with Bright

Star's copper-tinted logo. He and Joe used the pickups to haul maintenance and groundskeeping tools, cleaning supplies, firewood, and anything else that needed hauling.

Simon pointed the truck down the road that led away from the office and turned left at the side road just two-hundred yards from Bright Star's gate. A minute later he parked at the Mitchells' cabin. His own cabin, once the bunkhouse of the stable hands who'd worked for Joe's grandparents' summer camp, was off the next turn down the road.

Holly had left the front door unlocked, so Simon didn't knock. He went inside, stood in the small living room, and listened. All was quiet. He turned his head, still listening. There it was: the breathy in-and-out sounds of deep sleep coming from the second bedroom.

Simon tried the bedroom door, but as Holly had told him, it was locked. *Just a push-button knob lock. No need to break anything.*

Simon pulled his Allen wrench multi-tool from its pouch on his belt, selected its thinnest wrench, and inserted it into the hole in the knob to pop the lock. He stood in the open doorway and surveyed the room, starting with Skipper. The kid lay on his belly under a wild tangle of covers, his head on a fluffy pillow, face turned to the side, one arm dangling over the side of the bed.

Ah, youth! Sleeping on my stomach with my head angled like that would give me an all-day crick in the neck—sort of like the pain in the neck this kid is.

He turned his attention on the room. Discarded clothes, crumbs, crumpled candy wrappers, empty soda cans, and an open bag of chips littered the floor.

Simon spoke aloud with blatant disregard for Skipper's state of repose. "This place reeks like a pigsty. No wonder Holly doesn't think she can tolerate this kid's *disorder.*"

Skipper twitched. His tousled head jerked up from the pillow. He flipped over and stared around in confusion. When he spotted Simon, he sat up. The kid was startled, but he managed to cover his fluster with a challenge.

"Fletcher! What the *blank* are you doing in my room?"

"Technically? Not your room, Skippy. Belongs to your aunt and uncle. Oh. And I'd advise you not to curse at me. I don't appreciate it."

"Yeah, well, my door was locked! You had no right to unlock it and barge in here—and my name's not Skippy; it's *Skipper.*"

"Again, *not your room*, SkipBo. Belongs to your aunt and uncle. And since you didn't show up for work on time, your aunt gave me permission to roust you from your bed."

"I'm not working for them, and you can't make me. They aren't even paying me, and that's illegal. Now get out!"

Skipper grabbed at the covers, pulled them over his shoulders, flopped over, and buried his head in the pillow.

Simon took hold of the covers, and in one smooth move, yanked them off the bed onto the floor.

Skipper came up shouting, "I'm calling the cops on you, Fletch!"

Simon tossed the boy his cellphone. "Here. Use mine. You don't have one—and if you did? I doubt you could find it in this mess. By the way, while you're on the line with the police, don't forget to tell them the conditions of your probation."

That did the trick. Blinking in sudden uncertainty, Skipper sank in on himself.

Simon didn't let him stay there. "Get out of bed, nugget. We're burning daylight."

"My name is *Skipper!*" Under the outrage lurked tears.

Simon stepped to the side of the bed. "I'll use your proper name when you start holding up your end of the bargain. You agreed to the judge's terms, to his allowing you to come here instead of spending the summer at home under house arrest."

"Like I had a stinking choice."

"You had a choice, kid—in fact, you had several choices. Despite your mother's instructions, you chose to hang out with two up-and-coming criminals. Despite their bad reputations and the amount of trouble they'd already been in, you chose to pal around with them and follow in their footsteps. And despite knowing the difference between right and wrong, you chose to watch them start a fire in your school's cafeteria. *Those were the choices you made.*"

Simon picked up the half-empty bag of chips and squeezed the bag, crushing its contents to chip dust. Then he opened the bag and emptied it into the room's trash can.

"Today, you have another choice, *Skippy*. Get your butt out of bed and get to work or no food. Nothing. Not a bite."

"That's child abuse!"

"Good. We do agree on one thing: You, Skipperoo, are a child."

Skipper jumped to his feet, trembling with rage. "I am not!"

"As long as you behave like a child, you *are* a child, Skipperdoodle. And the judge's order dictated the conditions of your probation, not your aunt or uncle. You're to be paid for the work you do with room and board. Period. We're standing in the room your uncle has graciously allowed you to sleep in—*if* you work. Board means daily food. No work? No food and no expectation of privacy."

Skipper opened his mouth to retort, but Simon wasn't having anymore of the kid's lip.

He edged as close to Skipper as he could without actually touching him, standard military police intimidation tactic. He leaned in nose to nose, eye to eye, his countenance as fixed and unyielding as a rock, and roared.

"*Get. Your. Clothes. On. Nugget!* Now! Now! Now!"

Skipper withered under Simon's bellows. The instant Simon stepped back, Skipper grabbed a pair of dirty jeans from the floor and yanked them up and over his boxers. He scrambled for shirt, socks, and shoes, and pulled them on too. Uncertain what to do next, he slid a nervous glance toward Simon.

"Are you a human being or a dumb animal?" Simon barked. "Make that bed! When you're done, police this room, take out the trash, and get in the truck!"

Skipper hurried to comply.

Minutes later, with Simon nipping at his heels, Skipper ran from the Mitchells' cabin and jumped into the truck's passenger seat.

AFTER THREE HOURS of labor, Simon and Skipper reported back to the park office. They had hung all twenty-four site banners, cleaned the bathrooms in the swimming complex (not that they had been used or needed cleaning), wiped down the kitchen and other parts of the rec cabin—the bathrooms, game room, and gym, and swept all the floors. Outside, they had tightened the sagging volleyball/badminton net.

It hadn't been fun for either of them.

Simon had kept pressure on the boy the same way his unit's staff sergeant used to establish his personal and unit expectations and to ensure that the Marines in his charge performed to his exacting standards—until they did so without supervision. Regardless of the task at hand, Simon kept Skipper jumping and running, never giving him a moment's peace or rest.

When Holly came out of the back room that served as her personal office, she leaned her elbows on the counter between her and them and waited for Simon to report their progress.

He rehearsed their finished tasks, then asked, "What else do you have for us this morning?"

Holly looked from Skipper's downcast eyes to Simon and back. "I'd like a supply of firewood stacked under the rec cabin's eaves for use in the group firepit."

Bright Star had six cords of firewood stacked to one side of the office, along with a huge pile of kindling. Residents could pick up what they needed for their site's firepit at any time or request that a park employee deliver a fresh supply to their site.

"Can do. What else?"

Holly pointed to a rolling laundry bin filled with neatly folded towels. "Just finished folding those towels. Stock them in the swimming complex's changing rooms, please."

"Consider it done. Happy to help. Right, Skipper?"

Simon lifted his chin toward Skipper and waited.

"Um, right, Fletch."

Simon then tipped his head toward the laundry bin, and Skipper quick-stepped to the bin and dragged it toward the door.

"Well!" Holly breathed. "The age of miracles has not passed away after all."

"We're coming along," was all Simon replied.

"Good. Now get out of here," she tossed over her shoulder on her way back through her office door. "I have paperwork to do."

He followed Skipper and the laundry bin to the door and grabbed the bin's back edge, giving it the assist needed to propel the bin's wheels over the threshold and onto the cabin's low porch.

That was the moment a vintage two-door panel wagon eased to a stop in front of the office and Skipper and Simon's forward motion came to an abrupt halt. The passenger's side of the panel wagon faced the office, so Simon could not see the driver. Besides, he was too busy gawking at the car to notice much else.

"*Wow*," Simon exclaimed under his breath. He stepped off the porch to ogle the car up close.

The classic car had been meticulously restored, its body a deep smoky blue, the paint job exquisite. Every inch of the wood paneling that covered the passenger side of the car gleamed, including the trim that ran down the side to the car's rounded rear corner. Simon resisted the urge to stroke the blue front fender—that was a classic car "no-no"—even as he took in the car's shiny new tires and their wide, blindingly white sidewalls.

Skipper joined Simon in his examination of the car's hood. "What kinda car *is* this?" he demanded.

Reverence in his voice, Simon answered, "This, my boy, is a 1950 Ford Custom Country Squire—a panel wagon commonly known as a 'woody.'"

Skipper echoed Simon's sentiments. "Er, *wow*."

CHAPTER 2

SIMON WAS SO ENGROSSED in the details of the vintage vehicle that he had paid no attention to the driver, and did not readily notice when she got out and hobbled her way to the front of the car. Not until a quiet voice said,

"1951, actually."

Simon dragged his eyes off the car. Did a reluctant about-face, then swiveled his head left and right.

"Down here," the woman murmured.

He looked down.

The woman before him was short. Not merely short, but really short. Possibly inches below the five-foot mark—not that he, Simon, was any measure of "tallness." He compensated for his lack of height in muscle mass.

When the woman shifted a little of her weight onto a cane, Simon glanced lower. She wore a child-size "boot" strapped around her left calf, ankle, and foot, one of those stiff orthopedic walking contraptions prescribed post-surgery or after an injury to protect a foot or leg while it was healing.

His perusal moved back up and took inventory. An out-and-out riot of curling black hair sprinkled lightly with silver framed the woman's face, a face surprisingly unlined for her age.

Which I'd put in her mid-to-late fifties?

She'd somehow managed to juggle a can of Zero Sugar Cherry Dr. Pepper along with the cane, because about then she took a swig.

Gah! How can she drink that stuff?

"Happens to be my favorite. Probably drink three or four cans a day."

Simon mentally smacked himself on the forehead. "I apologize for staring, ma'am. Impolite of me."

He redirected his attention to her face, and found that *she* was studying *him*. Yet, when he looked closer, his brows lifted: Two dark brown orbs—not unlike two glossy Junior Mints—stared steadily at him from under eyelids fringed by thick, stubby black lashes. But it was the hooded, almond shape of her eyes that surprised him most.

"One-half Korean, father's side, legal immigrant, 1960."

Simon frowned. *I'm getting real tired of you reading my mind, lady.*

To change the subject, he turned his scrutiny back onto her car. "So, not 1950 but 1951, you said?"

"Yes. You were correct on the rest, though. It is a Ford Custom Country Squire."

"Well, it's in amazing condition. Did you—"

"Restore it myself? Yes, but with the advice and help of professional restoration gurus."

"And those whitewalls—"

"Custom refabrications of the originals."

"Custom refabrications must be—"

"Pricey? Yes."

"The wood—"

"Paneling? Mahogany trimmed in maple."

"The original 239 cubic-inch flathead V8—"

"With Offenhauser heads? Certainly. Precisely rebuilt, of course."

"Well, it's absolutely gorgeous—"

She tapped her cane on the road's asphalt. "Pardon me for cutting short our fascinating tête-à-tête, but is this where I check in?"

"Check in? Oh! You're our early resident? Miss Finch?"

She inclined her head. "One and the same."

Simon extended his hand. The cool fingers the woman placed in his palm were as diminutive as the rest of her.

"Simon Fletcher, Bright Star Facilities and Security Manager. I'll be parking your RV for you—"

Simon's tunnel vision and rapturous perusal of the vintage panel wagon had blinded him to what the woody towed behind it. He lifted his gaze to her rig and nearly choked.

It wasn't a motor home. Wasn't a fifth wheel or a luxury trailer. It certainly wasn't, per Bright Star's stiff standards, a qualifying RV of any type or model.

Attached to the bumper of Miss Finch's vintage vehicle was a travel trailer. The trailer's paint design was a unique and exquisite combination of cream, gray, and the same smoky blue as the body of the woody.

Unfortunately, the pleasing paint job could not disguise the unmistakable and commonplace outline of a seventeen-foot Casita.

Simon slowly ticked off Bright Star's RV requirements one by one.

Resident RVs must be a minimum of thirty feet in length.

Well, that's a fail.

Resident RVs must be no older than seven years.

I suppose it could *be seven years old or newer—but highly unlikely.*

Resident RVs must be clean and well maintained with no noticeable neglect, damage, missing parts, or discoloration to the frame or paint.

Okay, it passes that standard. Certainly has an impressive paint job.

But even if the trailer were new enough to qualify for a Bright Star berth, it was nowhere close to the required minimum length of thirty feet, and Holly would kick hard at that violation. Worse yet, common travel trailers in general defied the gravest of Holly's rules—unstated but implicit though that rule might be: *Bright Star was for luxury RVs only.* The park's rules and high-dollar season fees were all about ensuring that nothing of an inferior class take up residence within Bright Star's hallowed grounds.

Simon kept his expression carefully neutral. Nevertheless, as a Marine, he was well acquainted with that old, anglicized, and diluted military adage: *No plan survives first contact with the enemy.* In other words, whatever "special exceptions" Joe may have promised Miss Finch? In Joe's absence, they were unlikely to survive first encounter with Holly. She'd die on that hill before she'd allow Miss Finch's common little travel trailer to take up residence at Bright Star and besmirch its reputation.

As a further aside? Simon would take neither fame nor fortune to stand in Joe's shoes when he returned from Vegas with the pool pump.

Joe, you are a braver man than I am.

"Skipper?"

The boy gave an annoyed huff. "What now?"

"Run inside and let Holly know our season's first resident has arrived."

"Yeah, whatever." With an impatient sigh, he dragged his feet up the porch to deliver the message.

A minute later, he dragged them back. "She'll be right here."

"Right here" gave Simon the moment he needed to put his arm around Skipper's shoulders, pull him aside, and issue a whispered caution.

"Before Holly gets here, make yourself scarce, kid. The fur's about to fly."

"Oh, yeah?" Wide-eyed, Skipper retreated to the side of the office where he could duck out of sight behind cords of firewood should tangible fur actually fly in his direction.

Simon glanced back to Miss Finch. She seemed calm and unfazed, but she did push a wispy curl away from her eyes. She then reached into the handbag slung crosswise across her body and retrieved an envelope.

Simon slid his hands into his pockets and shunted a crooked smile in her direction. "Mrs. Mitchell will be here directly."

She returned his smile with a soft one of her own. "So I gathered," she murmured.

Simon saw something glimmer in those dark-chocolaty eyes of hers, and an irrational impression nudged its way into his mind. *Why, Junior, ah do believe thar's steel a-lurkin' behind them thar chocolate drops.*

He squinted. Shook off the cowardly impulse to join Skipper around the corner of the cabin to avoid the coming unpleasantness.

You're a Marine, Fletcher. You've waded into drunken brawls, put down raging riots, and faced enemy fire. Stand your ground!

He was instantly irritated when he found Miss Finch still studying him. "What?"

"How long have you been out?"

"Out of what?"

"Military. Marine Corps. Lifer. Separated less than a year ago, I wager."

"And who told you that?"

"You did."

Simon hoisted his hands to his hips. "Says *you*."

Carefully, she lifted her walking stick and pointed it at his head. "You're not yet comfortable with a fuller civilian hairstyle, but I imagine Mrs. Mitchell deemed the Corps' 'regulation cut' to be a bit off-putting to her upscale clientele, so she asked you to grow out your hair."

She pursed her lips, then added, "I take back the word *asked*. She made it a condition of employment."

Marines are the definition of stoic. They do not allow the unexpected to rattle them. Do not easily show emotion. Simon had spent twenty years plowing that particular groove in his brain's gray matter. Had it down cold.

"And you could tell all of that from my hair?"

"Not from your hair but from your actions. You drew my attention to your discomfort."

Simon felt weirdly defensive and off-balance. He was beginning to wonder if the lady was telepathic. He hardened his frown. "And when did I do that?"

"The three times your hand rubbed your neck and hairline since I arrived. You dislike and remain unaccepting of your hair's longer length."

Holly appeared on the office porch. She scanned the panel wagon and its towed burden. Her brows shot up. Her head moved slowly side to side.

"Oh, no. No, no, no. *No*. This will *not* do."

As Holly stepped off the porch, Miss Finch hobbled forward, smiled, and held out her hand.

"Good morning. Miss Finch. I have a reservation and am checking in."

Holly ignored the outstretched hand before her and drew herself up—not at all necessary as she had at least six inches on the smaller woman.

"Miss Finch, I am Mrs. Mitchell, Bright Star's office manager. I'm afraid there's been a misunderstanding. Since you claim to have a reservation, I must assume that you downloaded and printed a copy of the lease from our website, then signed it and brought it with you?"

Miss Finch's set smile did not waver. "Actually, Joe sent me a revised lease, one that made an exception for the length of my RV and that granted me an early check-in for today. He signed and dated the lease before sending it. I have a photocopy . . . if you're interested?"

Holly froze momentarily. Regained her chilly but superior demeanor. "Where is the lease with Joe's original signature?"

"Ah. The original, with Joe's handwritten revisions and dated signature, is in the safe within my RV. This certified copy of the revised lease with both of our signatures, thus a completely legal substitute for the original, is for your files." Miss Finch extended the envelope toward Holly.

Holly slowly took the envelope. "My husband mentioned that he owed you a favor, but in the thirty-one years we've been married, he has, not once, alluded to such a thing. I had never even heard him speak your name before he logged your reservation." She lifted her chin. "Just how do you know him?"

Miss Finch placed both hands on the head of her cane. "My acquaintance with Joe, although brief, goes back a number of years. We knew each other less than a month, and it was at the end of his military service during the Gulf War. You may ask him to share the particulars with you, if you like. It will make no difference at this late date."

Holly studied Miss Finch. "Joe was wounded in that war. He spent his last weeks of service in a military hospital in Germany."

The diminutive woman inclined her head once but added nothing.

Holly squared her shoulders and lifted her chin, her body language telegraphing her decision. "I apologize for the inconvenience, Miss Finch, but just as one cannot make a silk purse from a sow's ear, I cannot allow you with your, er, *travel trailer* to take up residence at Bright Star in blatant contravention of our exacting standards—standards all of our residents agree to and expect from fellow residents. I will discuss this situation with my husband when he returns from Vegas and am certain he will agree with me."

Miss Finch again inclined her head. "I understand your position, although I must reiterate that I hold a binding lease signed by the property owner." Her cordial manner remained fixed, even when she murmured, "Joe is, I believe, the property owner?"

Simon cringed. Talk about ruffling feathers! Miss Finch couldn't have said anything more contentious and certain to raise Holly's ire. He had heard the Mitchells argue over the issue of Bright Star ownership three times. Ownership of the *land* on which Bright Star stood had been Joe's tool of last resort when he was dead set against one of Holly's campaigns and was determined not to let her have her way. Sadly, that argument never seemed as effective as he would have wished.

Yes, Joe's grandfather had left the thirty acres to Joe as sole and separate property. On the other hand, the Mitchells had funneled their joint savings and other joint assets into turning the old summer camp into a luxury RV park. Nonetheless, whenever Holly pushed Joe for a decision he balked at, the issue of land ownership always came up. In those heated moments, Simon felt for Joe: It was the only card he had left to play.

The office phone rang, giving Holly a valid reason to break off the "discussion" where it stood in stalemate. She addressed Simon, saying, "Do not park Miss Finch's *trailer*, Fletch," as she swept across the porch and through the office doorway.

Simon cut a guilty glance at Miss Finch's back. He opened his mouth to—

"You need not apologize, Mr. Fletcher." She looked aside and sighed. "This is between me and Mrs. Mitchell. And possibly Mr. Mitchell."

Simon sputtered and snapped his jaws together. *She's not looking at me, not even facing my direction, yet she knows what I'm thinking?*

The woman turned toward him, the faintest of smiles tugging at her mouth. "My, my. Are you aware that you are rubbing your hairline again, Mr. Fletcher?"

Simon jerked his hand off his head and shoved it in the back pocket of his jeans.

At that moment, a shriek erupted from the office followed by Holly screaming, "Fletch! Fletcher! Help!"

Simon raced for the office door, catching a glimpse of Miss Finch's startled expression as he blew by her.

———————— ● ————————

HOLLY SAT IN A CRUMPLED heap on the stool behind the office counter when Simon found her. She was still on the phone, weeping silently, listening to the voice on the other end, and scribbling frantic notes.

When she gulped and demanded, "Where? Which hospital?" Simon reached across the counter, put a hand on her shoulder, and squeezed gently. She glanced at him, grateful for his comforting presence.

Finally, Holly hung up the phone and tried to pull herself together. "Fletcher."

"I'm here, Holly. Tell me what's going on."

She sobbed once. "It's Joe. A semi ran him off the road just north of Vegas, and his truck rolled over. He's got a fractured leg, possible internal injuries, and God knows what else! They're taking him by ambulance to a Vegas hospital. His truck is totaled . . . I have no idea about the pump."

She lifted her wet gaze to Simon. "Fletch, what am I going to do?"

"Which hospital, Holly?"

"It's . . . I wrote it down. Here it is. UMC Trauma Center."

"Okay, this is what you're going to do. You're going to get in my pickup and let me drive you down to Vegas." He exhaled slowly. "I'll track down Joe's truck and the pool pump. If the pump wasn't totaled along with Joe's truck, I will haul it back here ASAP."

"But Fletch, we can't leave! We have guests arriving tomorrow!" She stared at the binder on the desk holding the check-in schedule. "But I also cannot leave Joe, as serious as his condition is, alone in the hospital. I cannot! I refuse to! And if you drive me down there, I won't have a car to get around. Oh, dear. No, I think you should stay here, and-and-and I should drive myself—"

She ended on a choking sob, put her elbows on the counter, and dropped her face onto her hands.

"Holly, with the shock you've been handed, you're in no fit shape to drive. I will take you. I'll handle the details, too, get you a hotel room and arrange for a rental car so you can drive back and forth to the hospital. After we see how Joe is doing, I'll leave you with him and do my best to find the pump and arrive back here before noon tomorrow when the first resident checks in. I'll drive all night if need be. Don't worry; I'll take care of things."

The screen door slapped closed behind Skipper. He trotted up beside Simon. "Is Uncle Joe all right?"

"He will be," Simon murmured, determined to be positive.

As though Skipper weren't standing right in front of her, Holly groaned and whispered, "But what do I do with *him*, Fletcher? We can't leave him here by himself—the judge ruled he had to be under continuous supervision. Even if we *did* leave him here alone, there's no telling what kind of mischief he'd get into! I suppose we need to take him with us."

"Perhaps I can be of assistance."

Holly scowled; Simon turned around, surprised to find Miss Finch, both hands resting on the head of her cane, standing inside the office door.

"*You*," Holly ground out, "are not a resident and cannot stay here."

Miss Finch gently inclined her head. "Perhaps. However, I *can* supervise this young man while you are gone, Mrs. Mitchell."

"No! I will not allow—"

"Thank you," Simon interjected, cutting Holly off. "We accept your gracious offer."

Skipper protested. "What the hay? You don't even know this old biddy. I can stay here on my own."

Holly opened her mouth, but Simon held up his hand in the universal sign for "stop." Holly subsided before she could wind herself into a full fit.

Beside Simon, Skipper seethed. "I don't need a babysitter."

Simon answered the young man. "We talked about this back in your room, *Skippy*. Act like an adult and you'll be treated like an adult. Act like a child, and you'll be treated like a child."

Red-faced, Skipper protested, "Well, I'm not a child—I'm fourteen years old! The law says I'm old enough to be left alone."

"Yeah, you *should* be responsible enough to be left alone, which is why, when you aided and abetted your buddies in starting that fire, you lost both your credibility and your freedom. And just to point out the obvious? When your aunt and uncle agreed to have you spend the summer here, they obligated themselves to follow the judge's supervision order *to the letter*.

"Miss Finch has, out of the kindness of her heart, agreed to step in and keep an eye on you. You either stay here *and mind her*, or you ride to Vegas and back with me. Fourteen or more hours with me in my pickup, my choice of music nonstop, or remain at Bright Star under Miss Finch's supervision. Which will it be?"

Skipper growled low in his throat. "Stay."

"I need you to say that you will follow Miss Finch's instructions while I am gone."

Skipper cut angry eyes toward Miss Finch. "Whatever."

"Say it, *Skipperoo*."

Between gritted teeth, the boy fumed, "My name is *Skipper!*"

"Your name is *mud* if I don't hear you say *aloud* that you'll follow Miss Finch's instructions."

Skipper glared at Simon. "I will."

"You will what?"

His glare less pronounced, Skipper sniffed and muttered, "I will follow her instructions."

"Thank you."

"But I'll sleep in my own room in Uncle Joe's cabin."

"No. Nope. *Nuh-uh*."

Miss Finch spoke. "I have a table that makes into a single bed. Skipper is welcome to sleep there. All he needs is a sleeping bag and a pillow."

Holly found her voice. "But you cannot park that-that *trailer* at Bright Star!"

"Yes, I believe you made yourself clear on that point," Miss Finch replied, "but for me to keep an eye on both Bright Star and Skipper, it will be necessary for me to park my trailer somewhere . . . close by."

Holly huffed. "You may park behind the office. *Out of sight*. Plug into the outlet on the back side of the cabin. And Skipper may sleep in your . . . trailer."

"We appreciate your kindness and thank you, Miss Finch," Simon replied. "Will those arrangements work for you?"

Skipper edged in close to Simon and whispered for all to hear, "No way! Not sleepin' in some creepy lady's moldy old trailer!"

Simon pushed his face into Skipper's. "You'll do what I say you'll do or you and I will have another meeting of the minds, Skipperoni. *Do you get me?* When I return from Vegas, you can bunk at my place—top bunk only. No negotiation on that point. Until then, you stay with Miss Finch."

"*Fine*." Skipper subsided, but shot a dirty look in Miss Finch's direction.

Miss Finch.

Simon had saved his toughest words for her.

"Here's how it's going to go, Miss Finch. After I locate that miserable pool pump, I will break every speed limit between here and Vegas to get back before our first resident arrives tomorrow at noon. That said . . ."

He startled Holly and Skipper by stalking across the room to where the little woman stood near the door. He "gifted" her his most suspect-intimidating glare. "While we do appreciate your assistance, should anything shady happen while I'm gone, you'll have me to deal with."

It was said for Holly's reassurance more than any distrust of Miss Finch, yet Simon blinked in surprise. The cold, menacing face of stone he'd perfected as a military cop, combined with the sudden and blatant intrusion into the individual's personal space, had never failed to intimidate perps, young Marines, or most anyone else. So what was that twinkle swimming around behind that woman's two shiny brown orbs?

Wait. Where did it go? Simon backed up a step. *It was right there . . . and now it's gone?*

Unfazed and unintimidated, Miss Finch cleared her throat. "Right you are, Mr. Fletcher. I am accountable to you."

She then addressed herself to Holly. "Mrs. Mitchell, I believe we got off on the wrong foot. You must be terribly concerned about Joe. In your absence, please allow me to watch over Skipper for you while you see to Joe's care. And do not be concerned for your lovely RV park. With Skipper's help, I'll safeguard it today, and Simon has promised to be back tomorrow before your residents begin arriving. Please go, with peace of mind, and be with your dear husband."

Holly appealed to Simon, who saw the crusty shell around Holly crack. He nodded his approval.

Holly licked her lips. "I-I . . . well, all right. Thank you for your offer, Miss Finch."

"Not at all. Happy to be of service."

She pulled a business card from the handbag slung crosswise across her body and slid it across the counter to Simon. "I apologize for the crossed-out number. I have a new phone and haven't updated my cards. I've printed my current number at the bottom. Call any time. And your number is?"

Simon rattled it off. She typed his number carefully into her phone.

Then Simon gestured to Holly. "Grab whatever you need from your office. We'll stop at your place so you can pack a bag, but we leave pronto."

End of Sample

The TAHOE
MYSTERIES

ABOUT THE AUTHOR

VIKKI KESTELL'S passion for people and their stories is evident in her readers' affection for her characters and unusual plotlines. Two often-repeated sentiments are, "I feel like I know these people," and, "I'm right there, in the book, experiencing what the characters experience."

Vikki holds a PhD in organizational learning and instructional technologies. She left a career of twenty-plus years in government, academia, and corporate life to pursue writing full time. "Writing is the best job ever," she admits, "and the most demanding."

Vikki and her husband, Conrad Smith, make their home in Albuquerque, New Mexico.

To keep abreast of new book releases, sign up for Vikki's newsletter on her website, **http://www.vikkikestell.com**, find her on Facebook at **http://www.facebook.com/Vikki.Kestell**, or follow her on BookBub, **https://www.bookbub.com/authors/vikki-kestell**.

Faith-Filled Fiction™

www.faith-filledfiction.com | www.vikkikestell.com